The Red-Bearded King

A Medieval Legend

The Red-Bearded King

A Medieval Legend

John Eklund

gatekeeper press™

THE RED-BEARDED KING
A Medieval Legend

Published by Gatekeeper Press
7853 Gunn Hwy., Suite 209
Tampa, FL 33626
www.GatekeeperPress.com

Library of Congress Control Number: 2022941085

ISBN (hardcover): 9781662928208
eISBN: 9781662928215

Contents

Book I: The Ancient Kings   **7**

1. The Lance of Longinus 8

2. Henry the Fowler, the First King of the German Empire 13

3. Otto the Great 19

Book II: The Saga of Frederick Barbarossa
35

1. Lorelei 36

2. Gela 40

3. The Second Crusade 43

4. Crowned King and Emperor 48

5. Henry the Lion 52

6. The Emperor's Oak 57

7. The Holy Lance Obtained 58

8. The Pagan Rattenfanger on the Weser 60

9. The Wolf of Morbach 63

10. Krampus 66

11. Holy Roman Emperor 68

12. The Humiliation of Milan 72

13. The Doppelganger 77

14. The Battle of Legnano 80

15. Revenge Against Henry the Lion 84

16. The Crusade Against the Slavs 86

17. Hiedler and the Jews 91

18. The Battle of Iconium 94

19. Death in the River 103

20. The Kyffhäuser Mountains 104

Author's Notes   **110**
Timeline   **113**
Glossary   **114**
References   **115**

Book One

THE ANCIENT KINGS

CHAPTER 1
The Lance of Longinus

Whoever possesses this Holy Lance and understands the powers it serves,
holds the destiny of the world in his hands, for good or evil.[1]

In the Gospel of John it is written:

> It was the day of Preparation, and the next day was a High Sabbath. In order that the bodies would not remain on the cross during the Sabbath, the Jews asked Pilate to have the legs broken and the bodies removed. So the soldiers came and broke the legs of the first man who had been crucified with Jesus, and those of the other.
>
> But when they came to Jesus and saw that He was already dead, they did not break His legs. Instead, one of the soldiers pierced His side with a spear, and immediately blood and water flowed out. The one who saw it has testified to this, and his testimony is true. He knows that he is telling the truth, so that you also may believe.
>
> Now these things happened so that the Scripture would be fulfilled: "Not one of His bones will be broken." And, as another Scripture says: "They will look on the One they have pierced."[2]

The Holy Lance pierces the side of Christ[3]

1   Excerpt from the Spear of Destiny, https://www.kcblau.com/holylance/, retrieved 3-26-22
2   Excerpt from the Gospel of John. https://biblehub.com/bsb/john/19.htm, retrieved 3-26-22
3   https://commons.wikimedia.org/wiki/File:Hermann_tom_Ring_Kalvarienberg.jpg

The Roman soldier whose spear pierced the side of Christ was named Longinus. His is a name that all should know, yet few do. Even fewer know his story, or the remarkable story of his hallowed lance.

Longinus was a plebeian, a simple commoner in the vast and merciless Roman Empire. He was a physically imposing man, with dark eyes and a dark complexion, who hailed from Antioch in ancient Syria. His character was far different than what one would have assumed based on his profession. Longinus was trustworthy and brave. He was also goodhearted, with an affable nature, although not given to prolonged conversation. More than anything else, Longinus was pensive, and often looked to the sky. He was constantly searching for meaning in his life, but he never seemed to be able to find what he was looking for.

Like most Roman men in his era, Longinus dreamed in his youth of glory on the battle-field, but unfortunately for him he was afflicted with partial blindness. His poor vision kept him from being able to perform the duties necessary to be a great soldier of battle; so to earn his daily wage, he assisted in the crucifixions of outlaws and political heretics. He detested his profession, and felt very much like a prisoner himself.

On that fateful day in early spring of 33 AD, when Longinus thrust his iron spear, some of the blood of Christ splattered into his eyes. When he wiped his face clean on his cloak, Longinus was amazed, for he found that he could now see with perfect clarity. "Truly, this was the Son of God," he said.

Longinus resigned from his occupation as a soldier and became a Christian monk, doing good works for the remainder of his days. "His blood gave me my sight, but not only that. It gave me new life. I am now His humble servant, and I am more fulfilled here on earth than I ever thought possible," he said.

Longinus was martyred for his beliefs in the year 45 AD, as were so many other Christians at the time. He was hunted down and speared to death by the haters of the faithful in Rome, and his remains were torn apart by wild dogs. His death was witnessed by his brothers, who stood by his side and prayed. Many of these good men were murdered on the spot, but several escaped in dramatic fashion, racing in their habits and sandals through the streets of Rome. They ran not out of fear, but because they knew they had a task of utmost importance to perform.

Seven of the surviving brothers made it to their monastery ahead of their persecutors. They worked quickly to hide the Holy Lance, as the spear that pierced Christ was then called, for they did not want to risk it falling into the hands of sinners. They brought it to the catacombs far under the city, to a remote spot that only they knew existed. Four of them were eventually captured, tortured, and murdered. They could have saved themselves by revealing the location of the spear, but these were the most holy men of God, and they stayed true to their calling.

The remaining three recruited other worthy men to help them in their mission to keep the lance hidden until the day when a just and God-fearing ruler would come to power. "We will defend, and keep it safe, to the death if we must, like our brothers have done before us," they all vowed. This became the quest of the Monks of the Holy Lance, the name given to the order of the mysterious men who guarded the lance, and those who followed after them.

As the years passed, the monks needed to be more careful, for in that age of greed and hedonism, there was always the threat that one would give in to the temptations of wealth and security and turn against the others. They moved the lance from place to place, and no more than two at a time ever knew its exact whereabouts. They used secret codes and complex riddles to aid them in their mission, and they lived lives of harsh austerity and performed life-threatening self-flagellation to prove their faith and dedication to their quest.

When a holy member chanced upon a brother from a different fiefdom who he thought may be in the fellowship, he would pose the riddle:

> *"I never was, am always to be,*
> *No one ever saw me, nor ever will*
> *And yet I am the confidence of all*
> *To live and breathe on this earth."*[4]

If the brother gave the correct answer without undue hesitation, then he knew him to be a sworn guardian of the lance.

The Great Rulers

For centuries the mystical spear remained hidden, and it was nearly forgotten until Emperor Constantine the Great, an advocate of the Christian cause,[5] sent out a company of his most trusted soldiers to find its whereabouts in the year 314 AD. They had no reliable leads, and spent months searching throughout the Holy Land without any success. They had almost given up when one day they came across an old, grey-bearded monk in the desert. They did not tell the monk they were Constantine's men, nor did they divulge what they were searching for. Yet, the monk directed them to the underground chamber of a long abandoned chapel. He showed them a sealed wooden crate in the corner of the chamber.

---

4   Answer: the future. https://savagelegend.com/misc-resources/classic-riddles-1-100/, retrieved 5-22-22.

5   In the year 312 AD, Constantine fought a battle against his tyrannical brother-in-law, Maxentius, for control of the Roman Empire. The battle was fought at the Milvian Bridge, near the Tiber River. According to legend, on the eve of the battle, Constantine and his men saw a brilliant, shimmering cross of light in the sky that bore an inscription reading *"In hoc signo vinces"* or "In this sign you will conquer." Seeing this, Constantine ordered that the Greek monogram for Christ, Chi Rho, be marked on the shields of all of his soldiers. Bearing the symbol of the Lord, Constantine's army won an overwhelming victory, despite being outnumbered ten to one. Maxentius drowned in the Tiber during retreat, and Constantine became the undisputed leader of the Roman Empire. Having conquered "in the sign of Christ," Constantine credited the victory to the Christian God, and ordered the end of Christian persecution within his realm. In the year 313, the Edict of Milan officially ended centuries of horrific persecution.

"Open it," he said. "And you will find what you seek."

The men opened the crate, and found the Holy Lance. They were jubilant, but when they turned around to thank the old monk, he was gone. They never again saw him.

It was not long before Constantine held the hallowed spear in his own hands. With it in his possession, he reached greater heights than any ruler for centuries before or after. He ruled with justice and declared religious liberty throughout his empire. Ambitious and resourceful, the emperor's ultimate achievement was the founding of his namesake city, Constantinople. It would go on to become the richest and most populous city of all of Byzantium.

ΚΩΝΣΤΑΝΤΙΝΟΣ Ο ΜΕΓΑΣ.

Constantine the Great[6]

Constantine lived a long and fulfilled life. He was a righteous ruler who cared deeply about the destiny of his empire. On his deathbed in spring of 337, the God-fearing emperor decreed that the Holy Lance should be given to the pope in Rome, who he called the "Descendant of Peter," for safekeeping. And so it was. It remained in the possession of the popes for nearly 500 years, when in 800 it was given to Karl the Great[7] by Pope Leo III as a gift, soon after the wise and powerful Frankish king was crowned Holy Roman Emperor. Karl the Great carried the Holy Lance with him into battle forty-seven times, and was remarkably victorious on every occasion. With the lance, he was unquestionably the most powerful man in all the world.

---

6 https://commons.wikimedia.org/wiki/File:Constantine_the_Great;_the_reorganisation_of_the_empire_and_the_triumph_of_the_church_(1905)_(14587099818).jpg

7 Karl the Great was known as Charlemagne in France and England. Karl was also sometimes referred to as the "New David," because like David of the Old Testament, he was a warrior king and great champion of God's people. He was crowned Holy Roman Emperor on Christmas Day, 800.

When the great emperor fell ill with pleurisy and died at his castle at Aachen in 814, the holy spear was hidden for safekeeping by the pious priests of his kingdom, for the priests did not trust the morality of his quarrelsome sons. The Frankish priests, although well-intentioned, were not as dedicated to their mission as had been the Monks of the Holy Lance. The times they lived in, and the circumstances they faced, were far different than the draconian persecution braved by Longinus and his brothers.

Karl the Great (Charlemagne)[8]

8   https://commons.wikimedia.org/wiki/File:Charlemagne-by-Durer.jpg

CHAPTER 2

Henry the Fowler, the First King of the German Empire

Nimrod, the son of Cush and great-grandson of Noah (of ark fame), was the king of Babylon and erector of the Tower of Babel. He is the source of many stories and legends passed down through the ages. He was an ill-tempered and hedonistic ruler, with many wives and offspring. Other than his role in the hapless construction of the Tower of Babel, he was most renowned as a prolific hunter, and his palace was filled with trophies from his many hunts. Yet, it was not the trophies, but his powerful descendants who were the true prizes of Nimrod's life.

The Magyars

One day, two of Nimrod's favorite sons, Hunor and Magor, having the same passions as their father, set off together on a great hunt. Four days into their adventure, they spotted a magnificent white stag, running freely in the fields on the outskirts of their father's kingdom. They tracked the stag for three additional days, venturing past the outer boundaries of their father's realm. On the third day the stag led them through a marsh to a land well-suited for farming. There, Hunor and Magor met two daughters of Dul, the brave but merciless king of the Alans. Enchanted by the women's beauty, they took the daughters for their wives. Hunor's descendants were the Huns, the most famous of whom was the fearsome conqueror Attila, who ravaged Europe in the fifth century, and who went down in history as one of the greatest warlords of all time.

The attack of the Huns[9]

---

9   https://commons.wikimedia.org/wiki/File:Attila_et_les_Huns,_par_Georges-Antoine_Rochegrosse.jpg

Magor's descendants were the Magyars. Like the Huns, the Magyars were fierce nomadic warriors who heralded from the east, some say as far as Asia. They reached their height of power in the ninth and tenth centuries, and like the Huns before them, were the scourge of continental Europe. They rode swift horses and preferred the bow and arrow as their weapon of attack. They were greatly feared by peasant and nobleman alike. Legends claimed that they were only half human. Others claimed they were the Devil's army. It is true that they were a pagan race, who practiced shamanism and worshipped idols.

"We are cursed by the Lord, for the demons, spat out of Hell, fall upon us without mercy," one clergyman from Bavaria proclaimed after his village was terrorized by the Magyars. His thoughts were echoed throughout the German lands. It was truly a dark age for Christendom.

Rex Teutonicorum

For many years, there seemed to be no answer to the formidable Magyars. Fear and despair prevailed in central Europe. But then, in the year 933, to the shock and awe of all, the "demons from hell" tasted their first defeat in battle at the hands of Henry I, Rex Teutonicorum.[10]

Henry was known as "the Fowler." According to legend, he obtained this epithet because he was a passionate woodsman, and had been arranging his birding nets when heralds arrived to inform him that he was to be king. He was Germany's first true king, but had to struggle his entire life to put down rebellions in his kingdom and unify his people.

"United we stand, divided we fall," Henry proclaimed. "From the Rhine to the Oder, from the Baltic to the Alps, we are a people of God. May the Lord forever bless this land."

At the time, Germany consisted of four main duchies—Saxony in the north, Franconia in the center, Swabia in the southwest, and Bavaria in the southeast. The era was fraught with feuds between the noble princes, and until Henry came to power, there was no strong centralized government.

Henry changed the course of his nation. He was a deeply moral man with unquenchable intestinal fortitude. "I vow," he said, "to the King of all kings, to be a fair and gentle prince, to foster piety and the fear of God, to maintain peace, to further the welfare of this land, to help the poor and oppressed, and to be a righteous man and true protector."

Henry ruled from his castle in Memleben, in Saxony, and his struggles during his early reign made him proficient in the art of war. He began by venturing west, and routed Giselbert, king of Lotharingia, in the year 925. He then heroically expanded the German territories to the east, by defeating the Slavs in the epic battle of Lenzen along the Elbe River in 929. In that same year, he subdued the Bohemians by besting the noble Wenceslaus I.[11] Henry was aided by the

---

10 Rex Teutonicorum = the King of Germany.
11 This is the same Wenceslaus referred to in the Christmas carol "Good King Wenceslaus."

brave and pious Lohengrin, the Swan Knight,[12] of whom many legends are told. Henry later decisively defeated the fierce Danes and took the northern province of Schleswig. He went to war with the Danes to protect the many Germans in Schleswig from the evil new Danish king, Claudius, who had deviously poisoned his own brother to take the crown and queen.

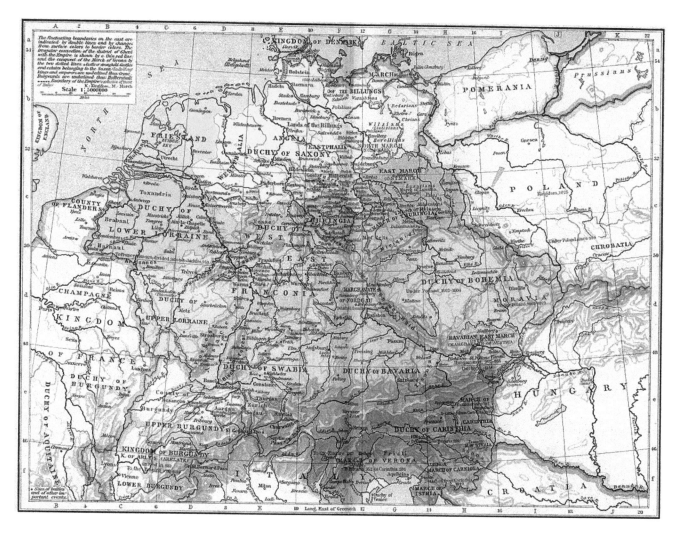

Map of ancient Germany[13]

"The state of Denmark rots under Claudius," Henry declared, prior to launching his attack. "We must secure justice for our brethren there."

Foresighted in the defense of his subjects, Henry established numerous fortified communities throughout his empire, called Burgwarde. Many of the Burgwarde evolved over time into towns and villages, including Leipzig, Meissen, and Brandenburg, and hence Henry achieved fame as the "Founder of Cities."

---

12 The famed Neuschwanstein Castle (translated, "New Swan Stone") in Bavaria was named in honor of Lohengrin.
13 https://en.wikipedia.org/wiki/Otto_the_Great#/media/File:Central_Europe,_919-1125.jpg

Henry the Fowler[14]

The Spear of Destiny

As great a warrior as he was, Henry knew he needed help if he had any hope of standing up to the nomadic army of the Magyars. A learned man, he knew of the Lance of Longinus, and ventured to Aachen, the capital of Karl the Great's kingdom, to claim it. "The lance is the key to our future," Henry proclaimed. "It is the Spear of Destiny."

Karl the Great had died over a century before, and most in his kingdom had either forgotten the Holy Lance or had brushed it aside as a myth for children. The priests who guarded it knew its value. However, as one generation gave way to another, they became corrupted, and they were not willing to give it up without great compensation. "The lance is worth twice its weight in gold," they told the king.

The wise and noble King Henry had two precious items to offer in exchange for the spear. The first was the jeweled crown from his own head, and the second was Hermann's Sword, the weapon used by the famed warrior Hermann to defeat the Romans in the Teutoburg Forest in the year 9 AD. Hermann was the greatest hero in Germanic history, and his sword was invaluable. The avaricious priests gladly made the exchange.

---

14 https://commons.wikimedia.org/wiki/File:Kaisersaal_Frankfurt_am_Main,_Nr._08_-_Heinrich_I.,_(Johann_Baptist_ Zwecker).png

Battle of Riade

For nine years, the Germans had paid off the Magyars with silver and gold so they would not attack and ravage their lands; but in the year 933, when the time had come to make the next payment, Henry left the Magyar chieftains a surprise offering—the rotting corpse of a dog.

"Treachery!" the nomadic chieftain cried out when he saw the dead animal. "How dare they dishonor us. Woe and death to all who resist us!"

With that, war was declared, and soon thereafter the great armies met at the Battle of Riade, on the Unstrut River, on the Ides of March. Although he had been defeated by the Magyars in years past, this time Henry had unfailing confidence, for he carried the Spear of Destiny before him into battle. "If God is with us, who can stand against us!" he cried out, rallying his men.

God was indeed with them. Led by their tireless king, the brave and determined Teutonic knights carried the day; and the Magyars, who had never before tasted defeat, retreated in terror and bewilderment from the field. Many laid dead, and many more bore serious wounds. For the very first time, the nomadic pagans knew what it felt like to experience absolute fear.

For the Germanic people, it was the first time in decades that the cloak of fear had been removed. "Henry has exorcised the demons," the bishop of Cologne proclaimed. "Thanks be to God, for we have been delivered from evil."

It would be twenty-one years before the Magyars would attempt to invade Germany again.

Henry the Fowler[15]

---

15 https://commons.wikimedia.org/wiki/File:King_of_the_Holy_Roman_German_Empire_Henry_I._the_Fowler.jpg

Henry had lofty ambitions, and dreamed of forming a new Roman Empire, but he suffered a stroke that left him dead in the year 936. He was loved by his people, and there was sadness throughout his kingdom at the time of his death. For seven days all wore black. For seven days none ate meat. For seven days all fires were extinguished. "God rest his soul," the people cried out. "We were blest to have such a man as our king. He was so strong. So kind. So brave. So just. We are forever grateful! Let us build an everlasting memorial to honor him," they proposed.

"He needs no memorial. His deeds are his monument," the wise and noble Lohengrin whispered poignantly, so that none could hear. He said this because he, having served with him in many battles, knew more than any how heroic a man the king truly was.

Henry was indeed one of Germany's great kings, but his eldest son, Otto I, would prove to be even greater.

CHAPTER 3

Otto the Great

Otto I was born at his family's castle in Memleben in the year 912. As soon as he could walk and talk, he was groomed to be a future king. He was twenty-four years of age when Henry suffered his stroke, and he had learned much about the ways of the world by the time his father passed. Otto truly admired his father, and was at all times grateful for what the noble king had done for him and his people.

"I pray that I may make you proud," he said every time he visited his father's gravesite. He visited often.

After Henry's death, Otto discovered that he had the same struggles as his father, namely a kingdom of rebellious princes who he needed to once again unite. Otto, however, also had the same aspirations and skills as his father, and he had in his possession the Lance of Longinus.

"With the Spear of Destiny, I shall found a Holy Empire,"[16] he declared to his people from the main balcony of his castle in Quedlinburg. "The Prince of Evil will untiring labor to corrupt us, and ruin us. Do not let him succeed! As the Lord proclaimed, beware of false prophets. And beware of false kings, who promise you glory but do not fear our Creator. The fate of Christendom is in our hands, and in the hands of our descendants."

Otto was a brilliant, resourceful man, with a stern demeanor but a good heart. He was ruggedly handsome, with deep blue eyes and a well-trimmed light brown beard. He was polite and witty, but seldom laughed. Like many Saxon men of his era, he was stoic, disciplined, dependable, and daring. None in his kingdom could outduel him with a sword, and none could throw a spear further or with greater accuracy.

"All beginnings are hard," the young king said as he started on the path to build his empire. Otto's first order of business was to tighten his reins over all of Germany as an all-powerful ruler. He did this both by force and through wise decrees. A God-fearing and just man, he allied his government with the church. Under Otto's rule, bishops were formally elected, attended court, administered the royal lands, acted as the king's diplomats and regents, and supplied the king with the bulk of his loyal knights. At its inception, his system was unique, but it was soon emulated throughout Europe.

Having gained initial success, Otto became bolder and more determined in his quest to create the great, noble and holy German Empire. He did not hide his ambitions, and his honorable contemporaries heeded his words with respect. His enemies heeded them with trepidation. "I look upon the people of this nation, as handed on to me, as a responsibility conferred upon me

---

16 Otto I, not Charlemagne, was the true founder of the Holy Roman Empire in 962. The empire lasted until 1806, when Napoleon Bonaparte, in possession of the Holy Lance, dissolved it.

by God, and I believe, as written in the Bible, that it is my duty to increase this heritage for which one day I shall be called upon to give an account," Otto proclaimed. "Whoever tries to interfere with my task, I shall crush!"

Otto the Great[17]

A Brother's Treachery

In the year 939, Otto faced his stiffest rebellion. His own brother Heinrich, several years his younger, was driven by jealously and sought to displace the great and noble king. Heinrich joined forces with Prince Eberhard of Franconia and Prince Giselbert of Lotharingia, the province that lay between Germany and France. The king of France, Louis IV, supported the revolt and supplied the princes with French knights as they went to battle against Otto. Leading with the Holy Lance, Otto routed his enemies. Eberhard died by the sword during the fight, and Giselbert drowned in a river while trying to flee. Heinrich was captured and brought before his brother. "You too, Heinrich?" was all Otto said.

Heinrich pleaded for forgiveness. "I have sinned against you, my brother," he said, kneeling before the king. "And I beg you for mercy."

---

17 https://commons.wikimedia.org/wiki/File:Die_deutschen_Kaiser_Otto_der_Gro%C3%9Fe.jpg

Otto was a kindhearted king, and despite his brother's misdeeds, he still loved him, and therefore he fully pardoned him.

Otto the Great and his brother, Heinrich[18]

Heinrich, however, did not learn his lesson, and in the year 941 he plotted to assassinate the good king on Easter Day in Quedlinburg Abbey, with the help of the Archbishop of Mainz. Otto learned of the plot, and his loyal knights again apprehended Heinrich and brought him forth for judgment . As he was betrayed a second time, Otto believed he had no choice but to end his brother's life. Filled with anger, he raised the Spear of Destiny, but as he gripped the holy weapon tightly in his hand, he heard a voice from above. "Blessed are the merciful, for they will be shown mercy," the voice proclaimed.

---

18 https://commons.wikimedia.org/wiki/File:Frankfurt_Am_Main-Alfred_Rethel-Die_Versoehnung_Ottos_des_Grossen_mit_seinem_Bruder_Heinrich-1840.jpg

Otto spared his brother's life, but had him imprisoned in Ingelheim. Heinrich remained in confinement for several months until a priest helped him escape just before the Yuletide season. Rather than go into hiding, Heinrich immediately made his way to Frankfort, where Otto was holding a festival. What happened next was a story told for centuries to come. On Christmas Day, while Otto was in the Frankfort Cathedral, together with hundreds of parishioners signing joyous hymns, Heinrich approached him, barefoot and wearing the hair-cloth garments of a beggar. He dropped to his knees at his brother's feet and pleaded for mercy. Seeing Heinrich dressed as he was, bowing before him in the winter's cold, Otto was deeply moved. "Bare is the back of a brotherless man," he said softly.

For a second time, Otto fully pardoned his brother, and from then on Heinrich served him nobly with all his heart. He went on to do great deeds for his kingdom, and himself became a hero of the German people.

Otto the Great[19]

19 https://commons.wikimedia.org/wiki/File:Otto_I_(HRE).jpg

Adelaide

In the year 951, Otto received a plea from a beautiful princess imprisoned in Italy. The princess's name was Adelaide, and she was from the wealthy realm of Burgundy, a province that lay between Italy and France. In the year 947, the sweet princess married Lothair, a handsome prince of Italy who was vying for the royal throne. Berengar II, the Margrave of Ivrea, was Lothair's ruthless rival for the crown, and poisoned the young prince three years after the marriage. He then imprisoned his bride in a dark, cold castle on the outskirts of his lands. He only agreed to free her if she would marry his loathsome son, Adalbert.

With the clandestine assistance of a loyal servant, Adelaide sent a message to King Otto, explaining her dire situation in detail, and ending with the sincere plea, "Help me noble King. You are my only hope."

Always righteous, Otto was appalled by the actions of Berengar, and sent her a simple message in return—"Dear Adelaide, I will be your champion."

Adelaide rejoiced when she secretly received the king's message, but she still feared for her life. She knew that Berengar would kill her if he found out she was the reason a German king was invading Italy. Therefore, with the help of her servant, she escaped the castle one evening and disguised herself as a commoner as she headed north in search of Otto's army. "I must find the King before Berengar finds me," she said. "Oh Good Lord in heaven, be my guide, be my light."

It was not long before Otto had gathered together a large force of brave knights and descended across the Alps to save the noble woman. The king and the princess met up in the Lombard capital of Pavia, and she bowed before him and gave him great thanks. Otto was struck by her unequaled beauty and sincere nature, and he took a knee and kissed her hand. "I promise you this," Otto said as he gently held onto her hand. "The day will come when all you see here will be yours. If you'll have me, then Italy will be yours, and Germany will be yours, Lorraine will be yours, and Berengar will be yours."

"I will be forever yours, good King," Adelaide replied, as tears welled up in her eyes. "May the Lord bless you and your noble men."

Soon thereafter, the German knights came upon Berengar's lands, but his cowardly soldiers utterly feared the tall and rugged Germans, and ran without a fight. Berengar himself was as cowardly as his men, and he hid in terror of Otto and his knights.

Adelaide[20]

Having fallen in love, Otto and Adelaide married on the 23rd of September that year, in a grand ceremony attended by all the kings and princes of Europe. The marriage was one of bliss, and there was true joy throughout the land for the next four years. The peace and joy were suddenly shattered, however, by the return of the dreaded Magyars in the year 954. The brazen Asiatic nomads began to ravage the lands of southern Germany, and even ventured as far as France, leaving death and destruction along their path. "The specter of Attila watches over and guides them," King Otto warned his fellow Christians. "Stopping them will be no easy task."

The Magyars were led by three powerful chieftains, Lél, Súr and the great horka,[21] Bulcsú. The three were all short in stature by Germanic standards, but sturdy. They had eyes as black as night, deeply tanned skin, and long, but thin, black beards. As did many of their fellow warriors, they wore the hair on their heads in a bun. They were ruthless men of war who lacked any respect for life and followed no moral code. They sought to avenge their forefathers and destroy the Christians. In particular, they wished to humiliate the son of Henry the Fowler. "Otto shall bow before us or die," they schemed.

---

20 https://commons.wikimedia.org/wiki/File:Abel_Terral_-_Sainte_Adelaide_de_France,_reine_d%27Italie,_impera-trice_d%27Allemagne.jpg
21 A horka is a Magyar general.

Battle of Lechfeld

In the summer of the year 955, Lél, Súr and Bulcsú began a siege of the village of Augsburg in Bavaria. The powerful Magyars expected little resistance, as Augsburg had no standing army. Yet, the Bishop of Augsburg, Ulrich, was a brave and brilliant man, and he led a courageous defense of his city, not clad in armor but in his priestly robes. He was unassuming, but spoke from the heart with true passion, and defended his village with true love.

Ulrich rallied his people with the 23rd Psalm: "Yea, though I walk through the valley of the shadow of death, I shall fear no evil."[22] Inspired by the bishop's spirit, the men and women of Augsburg grabbed whatever they had that could serve as a weapon, and fought with ardor against a far superior foe.

A messenger soon brought word of the attack to the king. Incensed, Otto hurriedly gathered his forces and prepared to journey to Augsburg. He did not fear the Magyars, but he did respect their military might. Although he had a much greater army, and far better resources than his heroic father did, Otto knew the Magyars too were far more formidable than they had been just decades before, and far more ruthless.

Otto was confident of the fact that his knights were the best trained in all the land. He lived by the motto "Practice makes the master." He himself followed this every day of his life, and he was a perfect example to his people. He was also very wise in the arts of war, and taught his commanders to be wise also. "Think first, then act," he told them. He emphasized the value of focus—"He who chases two rabbits at once will catch none, and he who defends everything, defends nothing." A practical leader, Otto made it a point to never complain, and to always make the best of the available resources—"Do what you can, with what you have, where you are. Crooked logs also make straight fires."

Otto was joined by all of his best knights, save his strongest and bravest knight, Gero, known as "the Great." Gero remained in the north, leading the ongoing struggle against the pagan Slavs. Still, Otto had with him Conrad the Red from Lorraine, and Berchard III, Duke of Swabia. Most importantly, Otto held the Holy Lance.

In August of that year, when the weather was brutally hot, it seemed like Ulrich and his stout kinsman could hold out no longer, but they were filled with heavenly joy when one morning the noble Berchard rode into their city, heralding the approach of the King. "Help is on the way," he proclaimed. "You soon will be set free. This nightmare will end. Glory to God and to our good King."

Otto and his knights soon appeared, and they quickly faced off against the Magyars and their three vengeful chieftains. The battle was not fought in Augsburg proper, but in the flood plains on the outskirts of the city, near the river Lech, in an area called Lechfeld. The titanic conflict began in the sweltering heat on the 10th, the Feast Day of St. Lawrence. Initially, there

---

22 https://en.wikipedia.org/wiki/Battle_of_Lechfeld, retrieved 4-2-22.

were heavy casualties on each side. The Magyars smashed through the Bohemian infantry that had accompanied Otto into battle and left not one man alive, but they were then beaten back brilliantly by Conrad the Red and his fearless knights. "The powers of Hell shall not prevail," Conrad called out. "Like Saint George, we shall slay the dragon."

Sadly, the brave Conrad was killed during the melee. The heat was so great that he removed his head armor, and was pierced by a Magyar arrow in the neck.

Battle of Lechfeld[23]

With the annihilation of the Bohemians, and the fall of Conrad, the hour of destiny had come. The Magyars, at last, met Otto and his main force of Teutonic knights[24] along the River Lech. They were not prepared for the fury they were to encounter. "Let us end this!" Otto proclaimed as he led his men into battle.

---

23 https://commons.wikimedia.org/wiki/File:Schlacht-auf-Lechfeld-Echter-1860.jpg
24 Here the term "Teutonic" is used as a synonym for "Germanic." It is not to be confused with the Order of the Teutonic Knights, which was not formed until the year 1190 in Acre, in the Kingdom of Jerusalem.

As the hot sun brilliantly illuminated the Holy Lance, the Eastern nomads were overwhelmed by the swift Teutons and forced into a haphazard retreat. Otto did not lead from behind as many commanders of the day did, but was in the middle of the fight. Although he carried the Holy Lance with him, his preferred weapons were the battle axe and sword. None were more heroic on the field than the great king. Over the next two days the nomadic tribesmen were completely annihilated. For the Magyars, it was a cataclysmic defeat. Lel, Sur and Bulcsu were all captured and taken to Regensburg, where they were executed.

Before their execution the three warlords were given the option to live, albeit as prisoners, should they renounce their pagan gods and embrace salvation through Christ. All three declined, and all spat in the direction of the cross in the town center in Regensburg as they were led to their death. "Those are the faces of the eternally damned," Ulrich commented as he witnessed their execution. "Lord have mercy on their souls."

Thus ended the Magyar threat. Never again did the pagans from the east venture into German territory. Widukind, the great chronicler of the era, recorded the events of the epic battle for future generations:

> "The next day, that is on the feast of the martyr of Christ, Lawrence, the King alone prostrated himself before the others and confessed his sins to God, tearfully swearing an oath: if on that day, through the intercession of such great advocate, Christ would deign to grant him victory and life, he would establish a bishopric in the city of Merseburg in honor of the victor over the fire and turn his newly begun palace there into a church. After raising himself from the ground and after his confessor, Ulrich, had celebrated the mass and Holy Communion, the King took up his shield and the Holy Lance and led his warriors against the enemy forces, annihilating and pursuing them till evening when they fled."[25]

---

25 David A. Warner, *Ottonian Germany: The Chronicon of Thietmar of Merseburg* (Manchester University Press, 2001), page 98.

The Savior of Christendom

Like Caesar returning to Rome after conquering Gaul, the victorious Otto was praised throughout all of Europe. Leading men and women came from far and wide with great enthusiasm to meet him when he returned to Saxony. He was rightly celebrated, for no other king in all the world had the skills and courage to defeat the dreaded Magyars. Truth be told, had it not been for Otto's stand at Lechfeld, the nomadic pagans would have overrun the entire continent, much as Attila and his Huns had done centuries before, and the course of Western Civilization would have been forever changed.

"Behold the Father of the Fatherland," the German people proclaimed. "Praise be to the Lord for the Savior of Christendom," the pious shouted out when they saw him pass by on his proud steed.

As he had promised, Otto issued a decree to establish the cathedral in Merseburg. It would become, for a brief period, the most sacred spot in the entire German Empire.

Merseburg Cathedral[26]

Battle on the Raxa

Soon after the great victory at Lechfeld, trouble brewed in the north. The pagan Slavs, under the rule of Nako and his barbarian chieftain Ztoignav, revolted and invaded Saxony, killing all the Christian men they encountered and enslaving the women and children.

Gero the Great and his fellow knights did their best to keep the Slavs at bay, but they were greatly outmanned. Hearing of the tyranny, Otto and his brave warriors marched north with great rapidity. They surrounded the pagans and offered them a fair peace, but the stubborn

---

26 https://commons.wikimedia.org/wiki/File:Kreuzgang_in_Merseburg_c1900.jpg

Ztoignav refused. Hearing that Otto's knights were exhausted from the journey and struggling with illness, Ztoignav plotted to make a stand against the German Christians. He retreated with his army across the Raxa River and made preparations for war.

Otto sent the brave Gero to offer the pagan chieftain one last ultimatum. "It should be enough for you, that you make war against one of us, one of the servants of my lord, but not also against my lord the king. What army do you have? What arms, that you presume so much? If there is any strength among you, or skills, or daring, give us a place to cross over to you, and let the valor of the fighter be visible on equal ground."

The Slav, gnashing his teeth in a barbarian manner and vomiting forth much scorn, laughed at Gero and the emperor and the whole army, knowing them to be aggravated by many troubles.

Gero was provoked by this, as his spirit was very fiery. "Tomorrow," he said, "will prove whether you and your people are strong enough in force or not. Tomorrow without a doubt you will see us contending with you. Tomorrow, before the sun sets, you shall know the wrath of my King, and you, together with your unrepentant warriors, shall burn in the eternal flames of Hell."[27]

On October 16, 955 the great battle against the Slavs began. In secret, Gero—who was as clever as he was strong—had had his men build three bridges upstream on the Raxa, so they were ready to cross and attack the pagans as soon as King Otto gave his command. And attack they did.

"The enemy is upon us!" the Slavic chieftains called out in terror early the next day. Believing that they were in a position of safety across the Raxa, they did not think it possible for the Christians to attack them so quickly in such great numbers, and panic rapidly set in. "Inconceivable!" Ztoignav cried. "How can this be? It must be sorcery."

The Slavs were no match for the heroic Teutonic knights. Gero himself faced the seven-foot giant Vlad, the greatest of the Slavic warriors, in a sword duel, and quickly triumphed over him. Seeing the legendary giant fall, many of the Slavs fled in fear. "Vlad is dead," they howled. "We are doomed!"

As he had at Lechfeld, King Otto fought with unparalleled skill and bravery, and his men were inspired to attack all the harder. The battle quickly became a rout in favor of the Teutons. Witnessing the Slavic catastrophe unfold before him, Ztoignav tried to escape, but he was captured in a nearby grove by a fierce knight named Hosed. "You often meet your destiny on the road you take to avoid it," Hosed said to the Slav, mocking him for his cowardly retreat.

That very day, Ztoignav was hanged for his treachery, just before the sun set. In his final moments, he looked to the west and bitterly recalled Gero's prescient words. His anguish could not have been more wretched.

---

27 Adapted from the historian Widukind of Corvey, https://themedievalelbe.uoregon.edu/battle-raxa, retrieved 4-2-22.

The Ottonian Renaissance

Having decisively defeated the Magyars and the Slavs within a three-month span, Otto was the most powerful king on earth. Jubilant celebrations for Otto's victories over the pagans were held in cathedrals throughout Germany. United as never before, peace and prosperity came to the German Empire for the remainder of Otto's reign. Religion, education, and the arts were of paramount importance to the great German king, and the glorious period of enlightenment that followed was rightfully called the Ottonian Renaissance.

Otto the Great[28]

Otto next turned to the south, where he crossed the Alps and went to war with Italy. After a string of victories there, he was proclaimed the Italian king, and soon thereafter Holy Roman Emperor. He grasped the Holy Lance in his right hand as the pope crowned him. "The days of battle have come to an end," Otto proclaimed, holding the Holy Lance high. "Glory to God in Heaven, and peace to men of good will."

Otto spent most of the remainder of his days in Rome. He did, however, return to Germany in 973, and had a grand celebration at his majestic castle in Quedlinburg. The celebration was attended by prominent nobles from all of Europe and the Middle East. It was the most talked about social affair in the entire tenth century, and served as a standard for comparison for all royal ceremonies for decades to come.

---

28 https://commons.wikimedia.org/wiki/File:Otto_I_Manuscriptum_Mediolanense_c_1200.jpg

Quedlinburg Castle[29]

From Quedlinburg, the good King visited his palace in Memleben, his boyhood home and site of his father's death. He suffered a fever while there, and died shortly after receiving his last sacraments on the seventh of May. He accepted death with honor and dignity. Quoting from the *Iliad*, he stoically addressed his children on his last day:

"Like the generations of leaves, so are the lives of mortal men. Now the wind scatters the old leaves across the earth, now the living timber bursts with the new buds and spring comes again. And so it is with men—as one generation comes to life another dies away."

Otto was the greatest king in the history of Germany, a man admired for his heroic feats on the field of battle, as well as for his just governmental reforms. Guided by the Holy Lance, and by his own noble spirit, he was the Arthur of his age, and all future German kings strove to follow in his footsteps.

"Otto, glory of the kingdom, born of the lordly lineage of his father Henry, and shining everywhere with brilliant deeds, thus ascended to the throne. At first, many evil men opposed him, from jealousy, but he conquered all their pride, with divine aid, which he sought always from on high. Since the death of Karl, there had been no greater patron, and I believe that the realm will not see a similar pastor again."[30]

—Thietmar of Merseburg

29 https://commons.wikimedia.org/wiki/File:Quedlinburg_Rehbock_Kurz.jpg
30 Warner, *Chronicon*, page 89.

Stained glass portrait of Otto the Great[31]

---

31 https://en.wikipedia.org/wiki/Otto_the_Great#/media/File:Bas-c%C3%B4t%C3%A9_nord,_baie_VI_Otto_Rex_(dernier_tiers_XIIe).jpg

Book two

THE SAGA OF FREDERICK BARBAROSSA

CHAPTER 1

Lorelei

Just as monks had hidden the Holy Lance for safekeeping after the deaths of Longinus and Karl the Great, the Holy Lance was again hidden safely away after the death of Otto the Great's grandson, Otto III. This time, however, it was not a holy man who hid it, but a man who cherished the welfare of the Germanic people, the noble Hermann of Bismarck, Otto III's loyal chancellor. Hermann was a Christian but seldom went to church. He instead often looked to the stars for guidance. He truly believed that the Lance of Longinus could be used or misused by powerful men, and that it could cause great triumph or unmeasurable harm, depending on who possessed it. He saw the decline[32] of his beloved German Empire unfold before him, and he made it his life's quest to guard the Holy Lance until a truly worthy man could hold it. At the time of his death, no one knew where he had hidden it. He had travelled extensively during the last years of his life, so the lance could have been anywhere in Europe, North Africa, or the Middle East.

In the middle of the twelfth century, there was one who was said to know the lance's whereabouts, a woman named Lorelei. She was an exquisitely beautiful but reclusive maiden who lived in a small shack next to a large rocky bluff along the eastern Rhine, in a place known simply as the Rhine Gorge. Some said she was a witch, others a siren, as she frequented the Rhine's waters, even in the cold months. What all agreed upon was her ability as a seer.

No one knew where she came from. She just mysteriously showed up along the banks of the Rhine one early morning. It was the day after a strange occurrence in the night sky. An unusually large shooting star with a long shimmering tail was seen across all of Europe. Many said it was an omen. The scholars in the era said it was the same star described by their ancestors in the year 1066, the night before the Norseman William the Conqueror launched his infamous attack against the Saxon King Harold Godwinson at Hastings, leading to the conquest of England.

One day an ambitious young man named Frederick, heir to the Dukedom of Swabia and nephew of the German king, set out to the banks of the Rhine to find the strange maiden, for he wished to know his future, and most of all he dreamed of finding the Holy Lance. At first glance, Frederick was not unlike other German men of his era. He was tall and fit, with pale blue eyes and sturdy features. His voice was deep and strong. He was courteous and good-natured, always making those around him feel at home. His smile was catching, as was his enthusiasm. What did stand out was his red beard, which matched the fire in his heart and soul.

Frederick's kingdom was to the south and east of the Rhine Gorge, a journey of several days. Although he thought it might be difficult, he had little trouble finding the mysterious

---

32 After the death of Otto the Great's grandson, Otto III, the Ottonian Renaissance collapsed quickly, leading to a dark and sinister age.

woman. When he arrived at the banks of the Rhine near the large bluff, he saw in the distance a stunning golden-haired maiden swimming against the current. "Lorelei!" he called out to her. "Come hither."

The exquisite maiden swam towards him and climbed atop a large rock sitting in the water, just a few feet away from the bank where Frederick stood.

"I am Frederick, the son of the Duke of Swabia," he said, introducing himself. "I have been looking forward to this day. It is my pleasure to meet you."

"Welcome, Frederick of Swabia, brave knight and future king," she said to him.

Lorelei[33]

33 https://commons.wikimedia.org/wiki/File:Lorelei,_A_Book_of_Myths.jpg

"King?" he questioned. "I am not in line to the throne of any nation."

"You will be the king of all of Germany," she said. She spoke in a way that seemed as if she were in a trance.

Frederick instantly believed her to be insane, but he decided to indulge her. "Shall I have a long reign?" he asked.

"Indeed, and a noble one."

"And how shall I die?"

"You shall die in a watery grave."

"Will I go to Heaven?"

"Yes, future king, you will go to Heaven, but not for a long, long time."

Frederick was about to walk away, believing it was a waste of time to ask her the where-abouts of the Holy Lance, but she stopped him before he turned. "The Spear of Destiny lies in Fafnir's cave, in the Gnitaheidr Hills of the Teutoburg Forest," she said to him. "Hold it with a pure heart, and you will follow the path to greatness."

"How long have you known that I've been searching for the Holy Lance?" he inquired, rationalizing that she must have been told of his mission by others.

"You are the first person I've seen since the solstice," she said.

Frederick stood silent for a pensive moment. He then took a deep breath in and exhaled slowly, maintaining an expressionless look the whole while. "Well, thank you and farewell, fair Lorelei," he said, bowing to her in a chivalrous manner before mounting his horse and riding away.

CHAPTER 2

Gela

Frederick was fascinated by his encounter with the mystical Lorelei, but he was soon distracted from his quest for the Holy Lance. One day while out hunting in the forests in his father's kingdom, near the Kinzig River, he saw a young woman his age with golden blond hair, enchanting red lips, and piercing eyes that were sapphire blue. She did not notice him at first, as she was happily gathering flowers in the meadow. "Those are lovely flowers," he said to her.

She was startled at first, as she thought that she was alone, and then she became more startled when she realized that it was the duke's eldest son.

"What is your name?" he asked.

"Gela," she replied.

Frederick struck up a cheerful conversation with her and found out that she was the daughter of a lowly serf in his father's realm. Her social status did not influence him whatsoever, as he fell deeply in love at first sight. She in turn fell deeply in love with him.

They walked together for a while up a path to the top of a small hill that overlooked the Kinzig Valley below, and then they sat and rested under an old oak tree there. The view from the base of the oak was breathtaking, and the warm gentle breezes on the early summer day made for a near perfect atmosphere. They made a plan to meet again in the same spot in one week's time, and they did so again and again all summer long.

The Emperor's Oak[34]

34 https://commons.wikimedia.org/wiki/File:Carl_Gustav_Carus_-_Memory_of_a_Wooded_Island_in_the_Baltic_Sea(Oak_trees_by_the_Sea)_-_Google_Art_Project.jpg

Fraternizing under the oak, they told each other cherished stories from their pasts and described memorable places where they had been. Being a peasant, Gela was not well-travelled, and she mainly listened to the tales of Frederick's adventures. However, despite her lower social class, she had a keen mind and remembered virtually everything she was ever told. Her learnedness was quite remarkable, and she often taught Frederick things he did not know.

"Hope is God's greatest gift to mankind," she once said.

"Greater than love?" Frederick questioned.

"Oh, love is marvelous," she said, playfully running her fingers through his red beard. "But hope is unsurpassed. Without hope, things would never change for the better."

Gela supported her assertion by quoting St. Augustine of Hippo, the renowned theologian: "Hope has two beautiful daughters. Their names are Anger and Courage. Anger at the way things are, and Courage to see that they do not remain as they are." Frederick always remembered those words, and often recited them throughout his life.

The Dream of a Golden Meadow

One afternoon, while under the oak, Frederick told Gela of a dream he had. "When I fell asleep last night, I saw us together, as husband and wife, in a kingdom surrounded by mountains, located on the outskirts of a golden meadow," he said. "A mountain itself was our august castle home. It was beautiful there. When the morning sun illuminated the meadow, there was an indescribably pleasing yellow glow. It was a land of warmth, and peace, and perfect harmony. We were so happy. It was so wonderful. I want that so much for us."

"But I am just a serf's daughter," she reminded him.

"I will renounce all I have, all hopes of power and greatness, to be with you," he told her.

Up until that time they had told no one of their love for each other, or the paradise they felt under that old oak. On the contrary, they did their best to hide it. Frederick passed Gela with cold indifference if he met her in the castle court, and Gela acted as if she was the unhappiest of his maids.

Faced with such a situation, Gela revealed their secret to the old retired friar from the village. He was a dear man with a pure soul, and she trusted his judgment. He knew both her and Frederick well. After hearing her story, the old clergymen gave her his honest opinion.

"Frederick loves thee now with the force of his unestranged affection," he said, "and is ready to sacrifice rank and worldly prospects for thy sake; but he is a man and a prince, and, above all, of the house of Hohenstaufen, in whose soul lies a longing after great and praiseworthy deeds, though these aspirations are lulled to slumber by his love for thee. But when he comes to years of manhood, he will be unhappy that thou hast kept him from the tasks incumbent on one of his noble race. And then, my daughter, not he alone, but all Germany will blame thee, for every far-seeing eye recognizes already in this heroic youth the future leader who is destined to bring this divided realm to unity and greatness. Canst thou think of the future of thy lover, and of us all, and yet act but for thine own happiness?"[35]

"No, my father," Gela replied in a firm voice, though the light of her eyes seemed quenched as she gazed at the priest. "No, I renounce him. But if he should ever think with bitterness of me, I ask of you that you will tell him of this hour, and why I have renounced him; because I loved his happiness more than myself. May this sacrifice not be in vain!"[36] Heartbroken, she set out the next day to a nunnery and dedicated her life to God.

Returning from a three-week hunting expedition, Frederick went to Gela's modest home to call on her. It looked different than it had just three weeks before, because there were no flowers adorning the boxes below the windows, and the area looked to be in disarray. Frederick immediately dismounted and called out for his love, but she did not come.

Then Frederick looked in the window and saw her father looking forlorn. "She is gone," her father said to him.

"Gone? Gone where?"

"She has joined the Sisters of Saint Clarissa, and has chosen a life of prayer and solitude. We will never see her sweet smile again," the peasant man said as tears welled up in his eyes.

Frederick knew at once the profound significance of Gela's actions. She had made a solemn, unbreakable vow to God, and neither bishop nor king could ever change that now. "But why?" he cried out, deeply distraught. "Why would she do so, without even the simplest of goodbyes?"

Gela's dear father was too overcome by his own sadness to take note of Frederick's. Gela had never revealed to him the details of her relationship with the chivalrous young duke.

With pain in his heart, Frederick sprang into his horse's saddle, cast a last glance on the desolate home, and then turned without a word of farewell to take the road which, but a short time before, he had galloped over with hope and abounding joy. "I shall never love again," he whispered to himself as a single tear ever so slowly made its way down his cheek.

---

35 https://www.gutenberg.org/files/39560/39560-h/39560-h.htm, retrieved 3-27-22.
36 https://www.gutenberg.org/files/39560/39560-h/39560-h.htm, retrieved 3-27-22.

CHAPTER 3

The Second Crusade

In the year 1146, the renowned French abbot Bernard of Clairvaux, backed by the French king Louis VII, called on the Christians of Europe to go on a crusade against the Turks to recapture the fallen province of Edessa,[37] which had been conquered by the Muslim warlord Imad al-Din Zengi in 1144. Konrad III, the king of Germany, heeded the call and gathered an army of knights to join him on a far-off quest to the Middle East.

The Monastery at Adrianople

The brave knights passed through the Byzantine Empire[38] on their way to the Holy Land. Although Christians, there were many unscrupulous monks and nobles among the Byzantines, who committed many ungodly acts. One of the greatest atrocities occurred when a young German knight sought refuge one evening at the Monastery of Adrianople. Instead of granting the Christian knight shelter and food, the greedy monks robbed and murdered him. When King Konrad heard of the horror, he was outraged. He immediately called on Frederick, for Frederick was his bravest and fiercest warrior. "I bade you to go into Adrianople and make justice," the king said to him.

"I swear by my beard. I shall avenge him!" Frederick promised.

Avenge him he indeed did. Frederick and his band of loyal followers went to the monastery, captured the monks, sentenced them in front of citizens there, and executed them. This to Frederick, however, was not enough to exact justice for the evil. The noble knight, together with his men, then razed the monastery to the ground. Not a stone was left unturned.

Justice was served. It was Frederick's first of countless acts against the robber barons and greedy clergymen in his kingdom and abroad. It was this unrelenting pursuit of justice that made Frederick loved by his people, and that formed the basis for the legends of his life that followed.

The Ark of the Covenant

Not long thereafter, Frederick and his knights came to the outskirts of Constantinople. It was September 1147. Here Frederick met a very curious dark-eyed German monk, clothed in a scarlet habit, named Astaroth, who claimed he had discovered the whereabouts of the Ark of the Covenant, the holy chest that held as its contents the sacred artifacts of the ancient Jews. He disclosed to Frederick the details of the findings that led to his discovery. Frederick listened with fascination.

The monk then put forth a proposition. "We could use the service of you and your men, noble Duke, to help us excavate the Ark," he said with a lisp. "It would be an honorable task, for the glory of God." He did not look Frederick in the eye when he spoke.

"It would be honorable indeed," replied Frederick. "But I can only spare three days. As you well know, we are on a mission of great import."

"Oh, much can be done in three days," Astaroth confirmed, his voice almost a hiss. "That, I can assure you, will be sufficient, noble Duke."

Frederick sensed a deviousness about the monk and the reticent men that followed him, although he could not pinpoint why. Nevertheless, he was deeply intrigued by Astaroth's detailed and seemingly incontrovertible findings, and planned to set out the next day to find the Ark. However, that night there was a torrential rain, the likes of which had not been seen in over five hundred years. The rain caused a great flood that swept away the mysterious monk and his men. The next day there was no trace of them, or any of their belongings. It was as if they had never been. "Incredible," the red-bearded Swabian declared as he looked about. "There is nothing as far as the eye can see."

Frederick had set his camp at the summit of a high hill and was unharmed by the flood, but his hopes of finding the sacred Ark were dashed. "Perhaps the Lord does not wish it to be found," he surmised as he gazed upward toward heaven.

The Ark of the Covenant[39]

39 https://commons.wikimedia.org/wiki/File:Joshua_passing_the_River_Jordan_with_the_Ark_of_the_Covenant_ (cropped).jpg

When Frederick reached the Holy Land, he found that the Christian army there was in disarray. To his surprise, many of the knights were not proper men of God, but ruffian drunkards who indiscriminately plundered friend or foe in search of nothing but wealth and glory. Few of them obeyed orders, and even fewer were competent enough to give orders. Frederick was quick to learn that the war against the formidable Saracens[40] was not going well. The biggest obstacle of all was the lack of support, if not sheer treachery, of the Eastern Christians—men who were supposed to be their biggest supporters, but who turned out to be unscrupulous backstabbers. Frederick did his best to right the wrongs of his fellow knights, but it was an uphill battle.

The Mark of the Beast

There was one Saracen who was so feared by the Christian forces that all would flee when they saw him approach the field of battle. They did not know his name, but the Christians referred to him as the "Man with the Mark." He earned the sobriquet because he had the Mark of the Beast tattooed on his devilish, red-painted face. Clothed in jet-black attire save a scarlet sash, he did not dress or act like the other Muslims. Rumor had it that he did not profess faith in Mohammed's God, but rather was driven to fight by his pure hatred of the Christians and their God. The Man with the Mark was ruthless in battle, and had no fear. He had no mercy either. After the Christians retreated, he searched the desert for injured knights and had them tortured and killed.

"He's a man possessed," one knight told Frederick.

"No, he is the Devil himself," said another.

"I fear no man, possessed or not," said Frederick. "I will face him in battle, and if he is the Devil, then God be with me."

The day came when the two warriors did clash. It was a Sunday. The Man with the Mark often led hit-and-run attacks on Sundays because he knew it was a day of rest and worship for the knights. A sentry outside of Frederick's camp announced that the Saracens were coming, but did so just moments before they arrived. Frederick quickly grabbed his sword but had not the time to put on his battle armor. He rallied his knights to fight with a call of "Unity, Justice and Freedom!" Bravely, he held his ground as the Saracens pillaged his camp. Seeing that Frederick had cut down many of his comrades, the dark and mysterious Man with the Mark dismounted his horse and approached him with his curved sword drawn. He called out to Frederick in perfect German, "Your God can not save you now!"

"Back to Hell with you," Frederick retorted.

In an instant their swords clashed. Both men were strong, and both were quick. Both were well-versed in the art of war. They whirled and struck at each other time and again, and neither seemed to have the upper hand. The day was hot and the sun brutal overhead, but neither seemed to tire.

---

40 Archaic term for the Muslim warriors.

Then, Frederick called out in prayer: "O Prince of Heavenly Hosts, by the power of God, thrust into Hell Satan, and all the evil spirits, who prowl about the earth seeking the ruin of souls!" With that, they clashed yet again, but this time the Christian's sword drew blood. The Man with the Mark of the Beast fell to his knees, clutching his chest where the sword had struck. He cursed Frederick, this time in perfect Latin, and then he cursed the Christian God.

Frederick stood over him and replied sharply to his curse, "I believe in the resurrection of the dead, in eternal life, and in the never-ending torment of the impious." Having heard those words, the Man with the Mark breathed his last.

Word spread quickly of Frederick's bravery and prowess in battle. He soon became a legend among the Germanic knights for having defeated the Mephisthophelean fiend.

CHAPTER 4

Crowned King and Emperor

Despite being undermanned from losses in prior battles and rampant disease, Konrad led his ill-fed and physically exhausted forces on a siege of Damascus. Once again, the red-bearded Frederick fought valiantly. As succinctly noted by the famed medieval French chronicler, Gilbert of Mons, "Frederick is said to have prevailed in arms before all others in front of Demascus."[41]

Yet, one man cannot win a war. The siege was an utter failure, and after just five days Konrad had to call a generalized retreat. It became clear to all that the quest to regain Edessa would go unfulfilled. Many blamed the catastrophe on the sins of the Crusaders, but Konrad placed all the blame on his own shoulders. Although he himself had fought bravely, Konrad realized he had not adequately prepared his army for the task at hand, and he had not anticipated the lack of support from the Christians in Byzantium, a critical mistake.

After the major setback at Damascus, Frederick and the rest of the Christian knights returned home, defeated and disappointed. "As you see," Frederick addressed the German peasants in Swabia, "we do not return as numerous or as imposing as when we set out. It was then a godly sight to look upon—nigh seventy thousand heavily armored knights, not including foot-soldiers, riding to the Holy War. Hungary and Greece were astonished when they saw the array, and exulted over the certain destruction of the Turkish army. Oh, the treachery of these villains, who expected their deliverance at our hands and then placed almost insurmountable obstacles in our way!"[42]

The Death of Konrad

Konrad III, the truly noble but politically weak king of the German Empire, died on a cold and snowy February day in the year 1152. Frederick was at his side when he passed. Just before he breathed his last, the good-hearted king decreed that Frederick should succeed him as the German monarch. Konrad had a six-year-old son who was heir to the throne, but the dying nobleman knew that the German Empire would be overrun by greedy princes if a powerful king did not immediately step in to save it from a calamitous destiny.

"Waste no time arguing about what a good man should be. Be one," Konrad said with a slow and frail voice. "And lead our people to a greater destiny. I believe you are the only one who can do so. I pass my crown on to you, Frederick of Swabia."

Frederick was shocked and humbled by the king's gesture, and he accepted, but first his ascendency to the throne needed to be approved by the other German princes.

---

41 John B. Freed, *Frederick Barbarossa, the Prince and Myth* (Yale University Press, 2016), page 52.
42 Adapted from *Barbarossa Crowned King*, https://www.gutenberg.org/files/65142/65142-h/65142-h.htm, retrieved 4-9-22.

King Konrad III[43]

Frederick was a popular choice, not only because of his upright moral code and affable nature, but because he was a descendant of the two most powerful families in the German Empire.

43 https://commons.wikimedia.org/wiki/File:Kaisersaal_Frankfurt_am_Main,_Nr._18_-_Konrad_III.,_(Ferdinand_Fell-ner).png

His father was a Hohenstaufen, and his mother a Welf. The Hohenstaufens and Welfs had bitterly feuded for over one hundred years, each hoping to gain total control over the German lands, but with the union there was hope for peace.

In a full assembly of the princes at Frankfort-on-the-Main, one prince praised the heroic courage Frederick had displayed in the Crusade, another his judgment and wisdom, a third his knightly virtues. A fourth was confident he would shortly put an end to the long and bloody conflicts of the Welfs and Hohenstaufens.[44] After an uncontentious vote, the red-bearded Swabian duke was duly elected king.

The Emblem of the Holy Roman Empire of the German Nation[45]

44 *Barbarossa.*
45 https://commons.wikimedia.org/wiki/File:Silhouette_of_Holy_Roman_Empire.svg

At Aachen, the one-time site of the throne of the famed Karl the Great, on a perfect spring day in 1152, Frederick accepted the crown, proclaiming:

With divine help I will prove myself worthy of their confidence. The history of our people shows that the man who is called to high duties, and places his reliance upon God, is a safe guide and protector of the people, and such a one often accomplishes important results in a short time. The incomparable Karl the Great[46] united all classes of his people into a powerful whole, forced the most rebellious to recognize his authority, eradicated heathenism in a single generation, reformed the habits of the people by the glorious teachings of Christianity, and established a well-ordered Empire. At a later period, when princes failed to profit by what he had accomplished, when fraternal strife swept away the best and devastated the country, they suffered many years from the disgrace of it and bowed their necks under the yoke of the barbarous Magyars, until the matchless Otto came with all the old authority and the old virtues, and made the barbarians tremble at the very name of Germany.[47]

Portrait of Frederick I[48]

---

46 As discussed previously, also known as Charlemagne.
47 *Barbarossa.*
48 https://commons.wikimedia.org/wiki/File:Federigo_I_Imp_(BM_1866,1208.690_1).jpg

CHAPTER 5
Henry the Lion

Frederick was not the only powerful nobleman in the German Empire. There was another nearly as powerful as he, named Henry the Lion. Henry, seven years younger than the king, was equal if not greater the warrior, and equal in wisdom, but he lacked Frederick's chivalrous nature and his unquenchable thirst for justice. Most noticeable of all, he lacked Frederick's charm and good humor.

Henry was a tireless worker. "Poverty is the reward of idleness," he was known to say, and he was never idle. His superhuman work ethic kept him in perfect physical condition, and hardened him against any difficulties in life he faced, whether it be the fierce cold of the Saxon winter or the blistering sun in the Middle Eastern desert.

With the exception of Frederick, Henry helped the German Empire excel more than any single man in his era. He built many castles and fortifications, and he was constantly at war with the pagan Slavs, gaining new territory to the east for his fellow Germans. Henry founded many cities, including Munich on the outskirts of the Alps, and Lubeck near the rugged Baltic coast.

Most at home leading charges on the field of battle, Henry often boisterously proclaimed, "God is on the side of the strongest battalions" and "fortune favors the bold." On the evening before a conflict, he would tell his men that "Great things are achieved only when we take great risks." However, after his victories (and he was always victorious), he gave thanks to God, and praised his fallen comrades with a poignant verse: "And how can man die better than facing fearful odds, for the ashes of his fathers, and the temples of his gods?"[49]

Coat of Arms of Henry the Lion[50]

---

49 A verse by Thomas Babington Macaulay.
50 https://commons.wikimedia.org/wiki/File:Wappen_Schwerin.svg

Henry was the son of Henry the Proud, a prominent Welf. Brought up in a life of privilege, he was of such haughty disposition and so ambitious that he was generally disliked.[51] Yet, as he aged he became respected by all, and the respect only grew with each passing year. Henry was considered very handsome in his day, with steely green eyes and a well-trimmed dark brown beard. He was tall and had a muscular build. In stature, he was the epitome of a perfect Germanic knight. He also had a thunderously deep voice, and commanded attention not only throughout his dukedom but most especially on the field of battle.

The Lion and the Serpent

A story is told of how Henry got his name. One day while on a pilgrimage to the Holy Land, Henry encountered a graceful lion with a beautiful full mane, at battle with an enormous green serpent. The serpent had been in a fruit tree in a lush garden when the lion first approached. Hissing loudly, as if to mark its territory, the serpent left its perch and slithered towards the noble beast, lunging at it with his deadly jaws wide open. The lion, in turn, lashed out with his razor-sharp claws at the serpent's head. Neither had struck a decisive blow, but it was only a matter of time before their struggle would turn deadly.

Henry was suffering from thirst after a long journey that day, and was desperately in search of water. That is what first led him to the lush garden. Once he arrived, it was the lion's fierce roar that made him rush to the scene of the battle. Not fearing for his own safety, Henry drew his sword and joined forces with the lion, cutting off the serpent's head just as it was about to strike and unleash its deadly venom. After slaying the reptilian monster, Henry hurried to a spring that was near the fruit tree, and drank until his thirst was quenched. It was the best water he had ever tasted, and he thanked God for providing for him in his time of need.

When he turned around to leave, he saw that the lion had been standing behind him, not making a sound. To Henry's astonishment, the docile beast followed him back to his camp, and stayed with him there from that day forward.

---

51 Adapted from *Henry the Lion*, https://www.gutenberg.org/files/65142/65142-h/65142-h.htm#fn_6, retrieved 4-9-22.

Brunswick Castle

Henry's castle was in Brunswick, in Saxony, and on its grounds he had a life-sized bronze statue made of his famed lion. Embracing his epithet, Henry incorporated the lion into his coat of arms, and had caricatures of royal lions painted on the walls throughout his castle. As much as he was a great warrior, he was also one who appreciated the arts, and his immense castle was adorned with some of the best the German Empire had to offer. The majority of the works he kept on display, but a few that he valued most were stored in hidden rooms which could only be reached by secret passageways.

Much like the lions of myth, Henry was unquestionably brave and noble. His only vices were his great ambition and the occasional jealousy that stemmed from it. He was a learned man and a natural leader of men. Like Frederick, he too dreamed of following in the footsteps of the legendary King Otto. He took pride in the fact that Otto was a fellow Saxon. "Saxon blood flows through our veins, and makes us true men," he was known to say.

In the main hall of his castle, Henry had a giant painting of Otto, portraying the legendary king at battle in Lechfeld. It hung above the center stone fireplace, and was deeply admired by all visitors to his estate.

The Brunswick Lion[52]

---

52 https://upload.wikimedia.org/wikipedia/commons/1/1f/Braunschweig_Brunswick_Loewe_mit_Dom_im_Hintergr-und.jpg

The Wendish Crusade

In the year 1147, Henry led a Christian Crusade to the east, against the pagan Wends who lived across the Elbe River.[53] The Wends were a fierce warrior tribe that raided the Christian lands, kidnapped their women, and made slaves of their men. They practiced human sacrifice by fire, and were greatly feared by the Christians on the west side of the Elbe. "They are a scourge against God's people," Henry proclaimed, "but with this sword they will soon know the wrath of God."

Joining forces with the recently converted Norsemen, Henry launched a furious attack against the Wends, defeating them in battle after battle and giving them the choice of being baptized by water or by blood, just as his ancestors had by Karl the Great. Unlike the Middle Eastern Crusades, which ended in defeat for the Christians, the crusade against the Slavs was a great success, and soon many of the Wendish converts became the most devoted of followers of Christ.

The Greatest of All Germans

Frederick admired Henry for his fortitude and love of the homeland, and he made him the Duke of Bavaria and Saxony. Henry's territory was vast, spanning from the Baltic to the Alps, and he adored every inch of the German landscape. "He is the greatest of all Germans," Frederick said of him. "Destiny has been kind to us, to have him on our side, rather than against us."

Frederick pays tribute to Henry the Lion[54]

---

53 The Wends were from present-day eastern Germany and western Poland.
54 https://commons.wikimedia.org/wiki/File:Philipp_Foltz_Barbarossa_und_Heinrich_der_L%C3%B6we_in_Chiavenna.jpg

CHAPTER 6

The Emperor's Oak

When not tending to his many duties as King, Frederick ventured to the hill overlooking the Kinzig Valley and sat alone underneath the old oak where he had spent so many moments with his true love. So many times he recalled the happy dream he had had of their life together in their mountain kingdom. So much had changed since they were last there together. "Gela, although I am now King, my heart has not changed," he whispered into the wind. "And it never will."

Frederick cherished the old oak. It was a magnificent tall tree with a thick trunk. It was the first to sprout leaves each spring, and was last to lose its color when the days turned dark and cold, often maintaining its glory until after the solstice. Frederick also loved the pastoral land that surrounded it. It was truly a beautiful place in the rolling hills of his kingdom.

Peasants and nobles alike would sometimes see him sitting there, in the warm summer sun, as they traversed the countryside to and from his castle. They knew not to bother him in his sanctuary there. Frederick's time under the oak allowed him to clear his mind and plan his future. He did not want to just be another forgotten king, but a great king who would forever be remembered by his people. He dreamed of following in Otto's footsteps and reigniting the flame of the Holy Roman Empire. "Let me not then die ingloriously and without a struggle," he said, quoting Homer, "but let me first do some great thing that shall be told among men hereafter."

For the rest of his long, long reign, Frederick would occasionally return to the oak, even when his hair began to gray. Always alone, it was the place where he was most at peace.

Decades later, after Frederick had been crowned Holy Roman Emperor, the bards told the tale:

> Beneath the shelter of his favorite castle the Emperor founded a town, and named it after the unforgotten loved one of his youth, "Gelnhausen;" and when on his travels he came to the forest of the Kinzig Valley, he led his horse silently aside, fastened the bridle to a tree stem, and ascended the hill to the majestic oak. There leaning his head, amid whose gold full many a thread of silver gleamed, against the trunk, he closed his eyes, and dreamed once more the old delightful dream. And the people called that tree ever after "the Emperor's oak.[55]

---

55 The Project Gutenberg eBook of Fairy Circles, by Villamaria.gutenberg.org

CHAPTER 7

The Holy Lance Obtained

Frederick ruled from his castle in Swabia, the Hohenstaufen Castle. It was a magnificent structure that sat atop a high hill that overlooked his kingdom. It was the most beautiful edifice in the entire German Empire. The castle grounds were meticulously maintained by his loyal servants, and the castle interior had the utmost charm, including seven baronial fireplaces. Frederick treated all of his servants well, and was well-loved by them. He demanded chivalrous behavior from all in his court, and all complied.

The peasants in the surrounding countryside looked at that grand castle as a sign of goodness and hope for the future. It stood as a shining light in the darkness of the Middle Ages. The land there did truly seem to be blessed. There was a tall and sturdy thorn tree on the grounds that bloomed not only in spring but also at Christmas. And there was a proud albino buck, white as the snow, which pranced gracefully through the forests to the north of his kingdom. There was a warm, crystal-colored spring at the bottom of the high hill, which was believed to have miraculous healing properties for wounded knights. The food was plentiful, and there was proper shelter for all in the kingdom.

Hohenstaufen Castle[56]

---

56 https://commons.wikimedia.org/wiki/File:Hans-Kloss-Staufer-Rundbild.jpg

One day while walking on the majestic grounds outside the castle, Frederick recalled his meeting with the prophetess by the Rhine. "How could she have known that I would become king?" he asked himself. "Perhaps what she said about the Holy Lance is true also."

The next day Frederick set out with two companions, Rainald of Dassel and Berthold, both loyal and brave, to the Teutoburg Forest. It was a four-day journey on horseback through friendly territory. Excited by the prospect of finding the spear, they rode furiously throughout the daylight hours, stopping only briefly to eat. They rested at night and told stories by firelight, recounting battles and loves from their pasts. When they reached their destination, they felt overwhelmed and deeply discouraged, for the forest covered a great expanse of rocky outcroppings in the seemingly endless valley.

"All the rocks and trees look the same, and there are many caves," Rainald commented.

"How will we ever know where to look?" Berthold asked.

The task certainly seemed daunting. Still, they ventured deeper and deeper into the thick forest, entering ten different caves and finding only darkness and bats. Soon the day grew late and the sun began its descent.

"We must turn back," said Rainald, "or we will need to make camp here in the dark."

"Just a little further," said Frederick. "In my heart I sense that we are near."

Then, as they walked along a small rocky stream down the trail, they saw a large boulder near the opening to a deep cavern. The trees of the forest shaded the boulder in such a way that the sun's rays made a perfect cross on the rock. "It is a sign," Frederick cried out.

In his excitement, the king was the first of the three to enter the cave, and sure enough, propped up against the back wall was a single lance. "It is here!" Frederick shouted with joy. "The siren's words were true! Praise to the Lord Jesus Christ!" He then dropped to his knees and closed his eyes in a moment of solemnness. "I promise, O Lord, to be a worthy steward for this Holy Lance, and to use it to serve your will."

CHAPTER 8

The Pagan Rattenfanger on the Weser

Frederick was always just, but seldom merciful. He had no tolerance for the many robber barons and other corrupt officials that populated his kingdom. When he passed judgment on them, he would sometimes spare their lives, but would always raze their castles.

One day while traveling with fifty of his men, Frederick came upon a quaint village along the Weser River in lower Saxony. It was an area not far from Hanover, but neither he nor any of his men had previously ventured there before. Within minutes of reaching the village outskirts he was approached by a forlorn farm woman. "Are you a righteous man of God?" she asked.

"I try to be," answered Frederick.

"Then please help us." The woman, soon joined by several other villagers, went on to explain that the duke of the village, a man called Rattenfanger, was the cause of her distress. She described him as a strange man, tall and thin, with sharp blue eyes but swarthy skin. He was conceited and wore brilliantly colored clothes. He also had a passion for music and collected expensive instruments from all over Europe. He heartlessly taxed the people of the town until they had nothing left, so that he may pay for his expensive tastes.

"When we could no longer pay, he took . . ." the farm woman could not finish the sentence for she broke down in emotion.

"He took our children," another woman from the town finished for her. She too started to cry.

"All the children of our village are locked away on his estate, serving as his slaves," a weary townsman added. He went on to explain that Rattenfanger was not even a nobleman by birth, but had obtained that position of power when he promised that he would rid the village of the plague.

"He came here with a mysterious charm," he said. "None knew his kin. Yet, all were impressed by his eloquent speech and colorful clothes. The duke of our village had died years ago with no heirs, and we promised to make him duke if he could rid us of the Black Death. He did rid us of the plague, but not through holy prayer. The man worships at the altar of Satan. And now he has my little Hans. I fear I will never see him again." The man too broke down in tears.

"I swear by my beard, with God as my witness, we shall return your children safely to you," the King vowed, as the midsummer sun began to set in the west.

Brüder Grimm   Der Rattenfänger von Hameln   O. Herrfurth pinx

Rattenfanger[57]

The next day was the Feast Day of Saint John the Baptist, and Frederick got up early and set off with his men to Rattenfanger's castle. Like the duke himself, the castle was draped in color. Brilliant flags flew along the grounds, and there were vibrant flowers in every window box. At the onset of the attack, as was his custom, Frederick held the Holy Lance high and shouted out his motto, "Unity, Justice and Freedom!" With the call, his gallant knights sprang into action. Rattenfanger's overweight henchmen tried in vain to resist, but they were no match for the King's mighty men. Breaking down doors and windows, the knights began to search feverishly for the godless sinner. Rainald of Dassel, blessed with keen instincts, found the colorfully clothed evil-hearted duke hiding, like a true coward, under his chamber bed. He pulled him out by his feet and dragged him to Frederick. "Shall we execute him?" he asked the king.

---

57 https://commons.wikimedia.org/wiki/File:Rattenfaenger_Herrfurth_5_500x798.jpg

"No," said Frederick, "but we shall chain him to the wall in the town center, with only his colorful clothes and his beloved flute. He will eat and sleep with the rats, and be treated as one of them, for all the rest of his days."

Then, breaking the lock on the gates with their axes, Frederick and his men freed all of the children, marching back with them in a joyous parade to their loving parents, who were anxiously awaiting outside city hall. A great celebration ensued, and the church bells rang from every cathedral throughout the lands that surrounded the Weser. "I have never seen so many happy tears," the king commented.

Truly in his debt, the townspeople sang the praises of the great king for decades to come; and each year on St. John's Day, they lit large bonfires throughout the village. They added a special mineral to the fire, so that the flames burned red like the king's beard.

Frederick with the children[58]

58 https://www.gutenberg.org/files/65142/65142-h/65142-h.htm

CHAPTER 9

The Wolf of Morbach

Even a man who is pure in heart,
and says his prayers by night,
may become a wolf when the wolfbane blooms,
and the autumn moon is bright.[59]

In the early autumn of that year, just as the last leaves were falling, King Frederick and his noblemen, Rainald of Dassel and Christian of Mainz, ventured to the village of Morbach. When they arrived they found that the villagers were in a state of intense fear. "Help us," a townswoman cried out to the king, "for we are all cursed."

The king and his men were confused by the strange outburst, until one of the town's noblemen explained the events that had caused the panic. There had been a town drunkard, named Lawrence of Talbot, who had a terrible temper when inebriated. Ever since his youth he had had an odd temperament and few friends. As he grew older, he developed an unusual reaction to the light of the sun. Wherever his skin was exposed to direct sunlight, blisters and then scars formed. Because of this, he ceased venturing out in the daylight. About the same time, he began to grow hair all over his body, including his forehead and nose. His temper grew worse and worse, and his behavior ever more bizarre. People avoided him as much as possible, but he was frequently spotted wandering around drunk, shouting obscenities to no one in particular.

The town's problem began one dark night when Lawrence, fully inebriated, broke into the home of Berchta, an old pagan woman who lived in a dilapidated shack on Haunted Hill, so named because the townsfolk believed that Berchta was a witch who communed with demons. Lawrence was in search of alcohol, having drunk all that was left of his supply. Berchta confronted him with a knife, but he wrestled it away from her and stabbed her in the abdomen. She did not die immediately, living long enough to utter a curse, overheard by her sister who was visiting her at the time. "You will walk this earth for the remainder of your days as a rabid wolf," she uttered. Those were her last words.

That was the last night anyone had seen Lawrence. Very soon thereafter, the villagers began to hear bone-chilling howls in the night, and would wake the next day to find their livestock slaughtered. Like a nightmare unfolding, villagers went missing, never to be seen or heard from again. There were sightings by the light of the moon of a giant wolf prowling the countryside. A terror spread among all, and no one in the town dared leave their homes after the sun set in the west.

---

59 https://en.wikipedia.org/wiki/The_Wolf_Man_(1941_film)

"We will find this beast and put an end to your fears," the king boldly proclaimed after hearing the villagers' tale.

"Beware, noble king, lest you become like him," a haggard old woman warned him. "You should be afraid, very afraid."

"Fear makes the wolf bigger than he is," Frederick replied.

The first night the king and his men set out to hunt the wolf, the king brought the Holy Lance with him. They used the carcass of a deer as bait and waited until late into the night, but the wolf never came. "It can sense the Holy Spear," the king said. "It will not come near as long as I have it."

The next night he set out with only his sword. Again accompanied by his loyal companions, the king waited for the beast under the light of the full moon. It was eerily quiet until just before the midnight hour. Then they heard a bone-chilling howl. Not long thereafter they heard a rustling in the woods, and then they saw it. Their eyes grew wide in amazement. Standing on its hind legs, the wolf again howled at the moon. Its height was over eight feet.

Frederick, however, knew no fear. He drew his silver sword and approached the beast. Rainald and Christian drew their swords also, but were not as bold as their king. They held lanterns to help guide Frederick through the shadows. The great wolf pounced, but Frederick dodged it. A second pounce was repelled by the king's shield. The wolf once again stood on its hind legs and howled, more loudly than before. Then came the third pounce, followed by silence.

At that moment in the dark forest, Rainald and Christian could not tell what had transpired, and their hearts raced. Then, they heard the verdict. "It is over," the king announced. "The beast is dead." As they approached with their lanterns, the king's companions saw the stab wound directly into the wolf's heart.

"It looks to be at peace now," Christian commented.

"Yes," said Frederick, "and now, too, can the villagers be at peace. Praise be to God, this evil has been extinguished!"

CHAPTER 10

Krampus

One early December day, King Frederick was traveling through his realm incognito, as he often would so to better learn the true nature of his rule within his kingdom. It was late in the day, and he was tired from his long journey through mountainous snow-covered trails, so he stopped at a peasant's home on the outskirts of the Alpine village of Garmisch to rest for the night. The home was owned by a kind man and his wife, and they had three young children. The man and his wife graciously offered lodging to the king, although they had no idea he was the king as he was dressed in plain clothes. Despite their kindness and generosity, Frederick could tell that the couple was deeply distraught. "What troubles you?" he inquired.

Tears filled the man's eyes as he answered. "The prince and his servants came by the other day to collect a tax. It was the third tax he has collected since the summer season. He took the few coins we had left and placed them in the sack he carried over his shoulder. He even took our only cow. We have no money. We cannot even buy food for the Christmas celebration."

"We at least were not tortured," the wife interjected. "Many of our neighbors were beaten until bloody with birch rods because they had nothing left to offer."

The king's blood began to boil when he heard the story, but he did his best to hide his emotions. "What is this prince's name?" he asked.

"Lucifer Krampus," the man answered.

"It's fitting his name is Lucifer, for he looks like the Devil himself," the wife added.

The next morning they ate porridge and prayed together, and then the king departed the forlorn family, never revealing his true identity. He raced home to his kingdom and gathered his brave knights. In three days he returned to the village and led his men to the grounds of Krampus's castle, which was on a small hill surrounded by a birch forest. "Raze it to the ground," the king commanded.

Krampus and his men quickly grabbed their swords and shields and tried to defend themselves. Krampus himself came face-to-face with Frederick. The evil prince did indeed look like the Devil. He had an unusually dark complexion for a native of that region. His eyes were bloodshot red, his tongue seemed too large for his mouth, his nails were long, and he had grisly features in general. His most astonishing characteristic, however, was his hair. The hair on his arms was thick, like the fur of a black cat, and yet the hair on his head receded in a way that looked as if he had horns.

Krampus's sword clashed with Frederick's, but despite his ferocious nature, he was no match for the battle-tested warrior king. Frederick's sword slashed across the monster's face, leaving a bloody gash. Seeing that he could not win the fight, Krampus ran from the scene. In the ongoing melee, he was able to escape, and was never seen in the region again. Nevertheless, legends of his devilish ways lived on.

A 19ᵗʰ century depiction of the mythical Krampus[60]

Before the sun reached its midday position, Krampus' minions were utterly defeated. Stone by stone, Frederick and his men razed the castle to the ground; but rather than keep the uncovered valuables for themselves, Frederick ordered that they be left in place so that the villagers could come claim them.

Late that evening, Frederick returned to the home of the kind couple and their three children. Doing his best to keep silent, he left three bags of his very own gold in the children's shoes that were sitting outside their door. Each bag contained enough money to purchase seven cows and a season's worth of seed. The noble king then furiously galloped away into the moonlit winter's night.

60 https://commons.wikimedia.org/wiki/File:Gruss_vom_Krampus.jpg

CHAPTER 11
Holy Roman Emperor

Having secured peace and prosperity in his own kingdom, in large part by waging open war against the many robber barons of his time, Frederick next turned south, to help the pope and to right the wrongs in the Kingdom of Italy. There was a powerful nobleman in Rome named Arnold of Brescia who was causing a disturbance. Although a Christian, Arnold greatly opposed Pope Adrian, and looked to overthrow him. Adrian sent word to Frederick pleading for assistance.

Frederick himself had reservations about Adrian; but being a dutiful Christian, he gathered a small army of knights and ventured south across the Alps to provide assistance. Travelling with him was Henry the Lion, the most battle-tested of all the Teutons.

One of his stops before reaching Rome was the city of Tortona, which had been completely overrun by a band of thieves and heathens. "There is not one good man left in the city," a peasant told the German king as the knights reached the city's outskirts. Upon entering, Frederick found the peasant's words to be true, as the city elders sent out thugs to try to rob him. Frederick and Henry quickly dispersed the thugs, but to them that was not enough. They sought justice. "Bow to the Holy Lance and submit yourselves to Christ, or face annihilation," Frederick shouted to his foes as he held the Spear of Destiny high above his head.

The miscreants of Tortona did not heed his words. Calling together their forces, Frederick and Henry destroyed the entire city, and sent all the heathens scrambling for safety in the surrounding wilderness.

For Peter, not Adrian

Weeks later, Frederick and his men arrived in Rome, and Frederick made preparations to meet the Holy Pontiff. It was a sign of fealty for kings and nobles to steady the stirrup of the pope's horse as he dismounted to greet them. When they first met, however, Frederick did not wish to be subservient to one he believed was a far lesser man, and he did not hold the stirrup. The pope treated him coldly that day, and it seemed like the planned alliance between the men would crack.

Frederick, however, was a fair-minded king, and did not wish to see his mission wasted over trivial politics; so at the meeting the next day, he dutifully held the stirrup, but whispered under his breath as he did, "*Pro Petro, non Adriano*" (For Peter, not Adrian).

Soon thereafter, Frederick seized the notorious rebel Arnold of Brescia and delivered him into the hands of the Church. As a show of thanks, the pope crowned Frederick Holy Roman Emperor at Saint Peter's, just as popes before him had crowned Karl the Great and Otto the

Great. Frederick was then led to the secret underground vault where the relics of the apostles Peter and Paul reposed. He fervently prayed there while a litany of joyous hymns were sung in the cathedral above.

Saved by a Lion

That very evening, a great uprising broke out among the disgruntled citizens of Rome. They were enraged that Arnold had been imprisoned. Several thousand Romans took part in the fray, and battled the well-trained and well-disciplined Germanic knights. They fought with vigor, and at one point even had King Frederick surrounded.

The Roman Revolt[61]

"It is time you met your maker," a Roman thug said as he raised his dagger and prepared to thrust it into the king's heart. But just at the moment he was about to strike the mortal blow, an arrow came flying at a rapid pace and struck him in the chest, killing him instantly. The arrow was launched from the bow of the great warrior Henry the Lion.

Henry then swept in on his steed, with the emblem of a lion adorning his shield, and like a true beast fought off the riotous crowd, saving the good king from harm. "Henry, I will remember it!" Frederick said to the Saxon duke. "You are a noble Teuton, and a true friend. I owe you my life."

61 https://commons.wikimedia.org/wiki/File:FEDERICO_BARBARROJA.JPG

"You are my king, and it is my honor to serve you," Henry replied, as he took a knee and bowed his head before him.

The Peace of the Land

When Frederick returned to the German Empire, he enacted a set of reforms known as the Peace of the Land. He also took a bride so that he could have heirs and a dynasty. The woman he chose, Beatrice, the Countess of Burgundy, was truly beautiful, a strong, holy and principled woman; but Frederick married to strengthen his political position, not for love. Nevertheless, he always treated Beatrice with chivalrous devotion, always faithful and loyal. The wedding took place at the cathedral in Wurzburg, and it was a grand ceremony. The poets described the new queen:

> Venus *did not have this virgin's beauty,*
> Minerva *did not have her brilliant mind*
> And Juno *did not have her wealth.*[62]

Marriage of Frederick to Beatrice[63]

62 Wikipedia, "Beatrice of Burgundy." https://en.wikipedia.org/wiki/Beatrice_I,_Countess_of_Burgundy, retrieved 4-27-22.
63 https://commons.wikimedia.org/wiki/File:Tiepolo_-_The_Wedding_of_Frederick_Barbarossa_to_Beatrice_of_Burgundy,_about_1752.jpg

Both the new queen and the Peace of the Land were very popular among the peasantry in the German Empire. The Peace of the Land in particular was greatly appreciated by the people, and made Frederick even more beloved by all. It consisted of a set of nineteen just laws, which were upheld by judges and defended by lawyers. It was a system much preferable to the old system, where might made right and justice was simply absent. The stated purpose of the Peace of the Land was thus:

> We, desiring the divine as well as the human laws to remain in vigor, do wish to preserve to all persons whatever their rights, and do by the royal authority indicate a peace, long desired and hitherto necessary to the whole earth, to be observed throughout all parts of our kingdom.[64]

King Frederick I[65]

64 Yale Law School's *The Avalon Project*, "Peace of the Land." https://avalon.law.yale.edu/medieval/peace.asp, retrieved 4-27-22.
65 https://commons.wikimedia.org/wiki/File:Pruddemann-Barbarossa.jpg

CHAPTER 12
The Humiliation of Milan

During Frederick's era, it was not uncommon for the larger and more powerful cities to take advantage of their less fortunate neighbors, either through forced taxation or outright pillage. One of the greatest culprits of the time was the city of Milan in Lombardy. They all but enslaved the surrounding cities of Lodi, Cremona, Pavia and Como.

In the year 1158, Frederick together with the powerful Henry the Lion again gathered their brave knights together and ventured across the Alps to right the wrongs in Lombardy. The citizens of Lombardy were descendants of the Swedes. They had battled south across the Roman Empire centuries before, and had helped defeat Rome. They were a tough and stubborn people, but at the time they were not well-organized, and were no match for the well-trained and honorable Teutonic knights. It was not long before the rabble-rousers in Milan were soundly defeated, and peace was restored.

One summer's day while Frederick was away, the city leaders in Milan got drunk and plotted against him. They made plans to humiliate his beautiful wife, Queen Beatrice. They seized her from her lodgings and had her ride backwards on a mule out of the city, laughing heartily as they watched her go past with her head down in shame.

It was not long before Frederick returned, and he was outraged by the injustice done to his wife. The city leaders tried to escape but were quickly apprehended. They feared death, but Frederick was a just man. No physical harm had come to anyone involved, and he did not wish to take a life over the matter. He did sentence them in front of the entire city to a punishment far more humiliating than that suffered by Beatrice. He led them to the yard where the mules were held, and made them eat the mud from the ground where the mules grazed. To further the humiliation, he made the Milanese announce "*Ecco la fica*," meaning "behold the fig," with the muck in their mouths.

In 1159, the nobles of the Italian city of Crema rebelled, and just as Frederick razed many of the castles of the robber barons in the German Empire, he razed the entire city to the ground. Those in witness of this were in awe, and many feared the Teutonic king. However, Crema was a relatively small city, and its destruction could not compare with the destruction of the great city of Milan that was soon to follow.

In 1162, the citizens of Milan broke the peace that had been established just a few years before, and brazenly denounced the emperor. A full rebellion ensued. Frederick once again gathered an army of knights and surrounded the city. As always, the red-bearded king carried the Spear of Destiny with him as he led his men into battle. "Unity, Justice, and Freedom," Frederick called out so loudly that those inside the city walls could clearly hear. Using catapults, attack towers, and battering rams, the knights stormed the gates and battled hand-to-hand against the defiant Lombards in Milan. The best of the Lombard warriors fell, one after another, to the swords and spears of the Teutonic knights. Soon it became clear that all hope was lost, and the chief instigators sued for peace.

The officials in Milan beg Frederick for mercy[66]

Tired of the insubordination, Frederick promised to enact justice. He was visibly angry and the people of Milan rightfully feared the worst. A feeling of impending doom engulfed the beautiful and proud city. A royal scribe, particularly moved by the palpable fear and deep sadness that surrounded him, recorded the events of the day:

Wailing and wringing their hands, the people prostrated themselves, begging for mercy in the name of Christ. Every one wept. Even the stern faces of the German knights were moistened by tears; for the severity of the penalty, richly as it was merited, touched them. The Emperor alone remained unmoved. Milan's repeated acts of treachery, and its lust for power, required exemplary punishment.[67]

"Repent, citizens of Milan. 'Tis better to be poor in honor than rich in shame," the king said. "Your lives shall be spared, but the city, with the exception of the churches, shall be destroyed. Lodi, Cremona, Pavia and Como shall perform the work, and you Milanese must find homes among these four cities."[68]

---

66 https://commons.wikimedia.org/wiki/File:Milan_leaders_surrender_to_Barbarossa_Year1162.jpg
67 Franz Kuhn, *Barbarossa* (Chicago: A.C. McClurg & Co., 1906). https://www.gutenberg.org/files/65142/65142-h/65142-h.htm#fn_6, retrieved 4-9-22
68 Kuhn, *Barbarossa.*

King Frederick I in battle gear[69]

The devastation soon began, and within days it was utterly complete. "A second Troy has perished," lamented the poet Godfrey of Viterbo when he witnessed the miserable ruins of the once great city.[70] To the forlorn citizens of Milan, the world had turned dystopian in the blink of an eye, but they realized that they had no one to blame but themselves. "This was the path of avarice," they bewailed. "May the Lord have mercy on us."

Joy in the German Empire

Upon his return from Italy, Frederick was hailed by his royal subjects as a great and just conqueror. There were celebrations throughout the land. Church bells joyously rang, and it seemed that all were in good cheer. Elaborate festivals were held at the picturesque Hohenstaufen Castle in Swabia. There were jousting tournaments and large feasts, with sauerbraten[71] and Schweine-braten,[72] bread with butter or lard, the best mustards from across the empire, and plentiful sweets, including doughnuts and fritters. The festivals were filled with bards who told fanciful stories, and roaming minstrels. They were grand events enjoyed by all, peasants and nobles alike.

The famed Bavarian chronicler Rahewin, in his biography of the king, recounted the peace and prosperity of the German Empire under Frederick's rule, proclaiming "Men had changed, the land had become a different one—yes the very heavens seemed milder and more friendly."[73]

---

69 https://commons.wikimedia.org/wiki/File:Friedrich_I._Barbarossa_(Christian_Siedentopf,_1847).jpg
70 Ernest Henderson, *A History of Germany in the Middle Ages* (George Bell and Sons, 1894), page 227.
71 Roast beef.
72 Roast pork.
73 Henderson, *Middle Ages*, page 222.

The Relics of the Magi

The twelfth century in the German Empire was a time of religious fervor. The saints were venerated and stories from the Bible were oft told, very often expanded upon as well. Among the many saints, there was a particular fascination with the three wise men of the New Testament. The legend arose that after bringing gifts of gold, frankincense, and myrrh to the Christ child, the three Magi returned to their far-off homeland, but they were forever moved by their experience in Bethlehem. Decades later, when they were long in the tooth, the three made a pilgrimage back to the Holy Land. They wished to see the site of the great star once more before they left this earth. Upon their return, they encountered the Apostle Matthew. Matthew told them the details of the life and ministry of Christ, and how he was born in a stable in Bethlehem. The Magi immediately recognized that Jesus was the infant they had visited. They were deeply stirred and publicly announced their conversion to Christianity, knowing very well that in doing so they would be martyred. They willingly suffered torture and death to embrace life in Christ.

The three Magi[74]

After their martyrdom, they were buried by Matthew, but years later, their bones were recovered and moved to Constantinople, where they were venerated. In the year 344, the bones were moved to Milan, as a gift to the city. They remained there for centuries, until Frederick and his men arrived in 1162. The German knights were careful not to damage any holy artifacts when they sacked the city, and the bones were secured and kept in good care.

---

74 https://commons.wikimedia.org/wiki/File:Magi_tissot.jpg

After taking leave of the ruins in Milan, Rainald of Dassel brought with him the relics of the three Magi and gave them to Frederick to honor the great king. Frederick was truly pleased. "We shall keep them here, in our land," he proclaimed, "that we may have a holy site on German soil, so that those too frail, or too poor, to venture to far off realms, may have a holy place of pilgrimage near to them."

The relics were stored in Cologne, housed in the magnificent Shrine of the Three Kings in Cologne Cathedral, and remain there to this day.

CHAPTER 13
The Doppelganger

Due to his military successes and his legendary chivalry, Frederick became famous throughout Europe. In the German Empire he was called *Kaiser Rotbart* (King Redbeard), so named because of his prominent red beard, but throughout the rest of the world he was known as Frederick Barbarossa,[75] the name given to him by the Lombards.

The Great Plague

In the year 1166, trouble again arose in Italy, this time in Ancona and Rome. Once again, Frederick gathered together an army and traveled south across the Alps.

While Frederick began a successful siege against the rebels of Ancona, an army of German knights, led by the gallant Rainald of Dassel and brave Christian of Mainz, went to battle against the Romans in the city of Monte Porzio, on May 29, 1167. The Romans were sure of victory this time, for they had amassed an army greater than any Rome had seen since the time of Julius Caesar. They were better equipped and better trained than any the Teutons had met before.

The day was a fateful one. Although greatly outnumbered, Rainald and Christian, attacking under the banners of the double-headed black eagle and of St. Michael the Archangel, led the German knights to a profound victory. The Roman legions were not just defeated but utterly annihilated. One historian later called the Battle of Monte Porzio the "Cannae[76] of the Middle Ages."

Although there was no army left in Rome to oppose the German knights, Frederick was unable to capitalize on the tremendous victory because his army was soon decimated by a horrific plague. On August 2, there was a violent thunderstorm, followed by an intense heat wave that ushered in the deadly pestilence. Even the brave and noble Rainald of Dassel, Frederick's most trusted chancellor, fell victim to the plague. "May flights of angels guide thee to thy rest, noble warrior," the king proclaimed at his death. "You will never be forgotten, my dear friend."

Having lost his army in a matter of just months, Frederick had to make a daring escape from hostile territory. Given the wet weather and the need to take obscure roads to avoid detection, the escape took many weeks, and the knights made many stops along the way to rest and gather rations.

---

75 Italian for Redbeard.

76 Cannae was a famous battle fought in 216 BC between Carthage, led by Hannibal, and the Roman Empire. The Romans were annihilated, and Hannibal's victory was viewed as one of the greatest tactical feats in military history.

Sculpture of Rainald of Dassel[77]

Hartmann von Siebenneichen

One day while resting in a castle in Susa in the mountains of northern Italy, Frederick and his small band of knights found themselves surrounded by a large mob, looking to apprehend and execute the king. The king was only saved by the bravery of Hartmann von Siebeneichen, Frederick's noble doppelganger.

Hartmann von Siebeneichen, like Frederick, had blond hair and a red beard. He was of the king's same build. He had only joined the king's band of loyal knights two years before, when he was discovered by Conrad of Feuchtwangen. The story is told of how one day, when the king was ill with fever, Conrad took off on a journey to find Hildegard,[78] a renowned botanist and apothecary from Bingen who was said to be able to cure any malady. While passing through a small

77 https://commons.wikimedia.org/wiki/File:RainaldvonDassel.jpg
78 Saint Hildegard of Bingen was a writer, composer of hymns, mystic, botanist and medical practitioner. She was one of the most remarkable women of the Middle Ages.

village, a group of six thugs stopped him and tried to rob him. Conrad was a fierce warrior and put up a valiant fight, but he was severely outmanned. Just when it looked like his life may be in jeopardy, he saw King Frederick approach with a sword in his hand, or so he thought. "It must be a ghost," Conrad lamented. "The king must have died of the pestilence."

Saint Hildegard of Bingen[79]

It was not a ghost but rather Hartmann von Siebenneichen, a noble knight with a pure heart. Hartmann helped Conrad fight off the six bandits, then joined Frederick's royal court.

Hartmann had saved the king's life by helping Conrad reach the famed Hildegard. Now, he was to save it a second time. Dressing in the king's garments, Hartmann posed as the Holy Roman Emperor while Frederick dressed as a peasant and snuck away with his fellow knights.

The Italian mob was so impressed with Hartmann's bravery that they spared his life and let him get away unpunished.

79 https://commons.wikimedia.org/wiki/File:Ildegarda_di_Bingen-wiki.jpg

CHAPTER 14
The Battle of Legnano

In the year 1173, Frederick received disturbing news. His loyal subject and comrade in battle, the powerful Henry the Lion, was oppressing his neighbors. He was calling for unreasonable taxation and confiscating the land of all who opposed him in the north. He did so to raise revenue for a larger crusade to the east. He wished to extend the borders of the German Empire, initially to the Vistula River,[80] but his ambition drove him even further. "I shall conquer an area greater than that conquered by Karl the Great," he plotted. "It shall stretch from the Rhine to the Dnieper,[81] and for centuries to come, all will remember and praise the name Henry the Lion. It is my destiny."

The archbishops of the beleaguered cities of Magdeburg and Bremen sent messengers to the king, begging for assistance. Frederick received them cordially, but was deeply troubled by their revelations. *Henry is the bravest knight and greatest warrior I have ever known*, he thought in anguish. *He was my most vocal supporter when the princes gathered at Frankfort-on-the-Main to elect me as king. He freely risked his life and saved me from the cold hand of death in Rome. If that were not enough, he commands the most disciplined army in all the German Empire. What am I to do?*

The king's anguish over the disharmony in his empire only grew with each passing day. "What troubles you so, my love?" Beatrice asked him one early morning, when he seemed particularly distressed.

"A house divided cannot stand," Frederick said to her. "I feel there is a cloud of doom over my kingdom. I had a dream last night that the Lord had forsaken me. I saw the sanctuary in the cathedral crumble to the ground, with a lion standing on top of the stones of the altar, and I saw you, overcome by sadness, clothed in a widow's gown."

"Why would He forsake you, when you have always done your best to serve Him?" she questioned.

"Maybe He is putting me on trial," he answered. "I can only pray that I am up to the task."

"It is always darkest before dawn," Beatrice assured him. "You will do what is right. And you will succeed. I know this in my heart. It is your destiny."

Although he considered Henry an ally, and although he owed him his life, Frederick was a man of honor and would not stand for injustice in his kingdom. He heeded Beatrice's words and traveled north to Henry's castle in Brunswick. By royal decree, supported by a strong show of force, he quickly ended the trouble. He then made all involved take a vow to keep the peace.

---

80 The Vistula is a river that flows from south to north in central Poland.
81 The Dnieper River runs through Russia, Belarus and Ukraine, and empties into the Black Sea.

Yet, Frederick knew that as a king, he could not be successful if he only ruled with an iron fist. He understood the value in compromise and in making concessions. He thus judiciously gave his verbal support to Henry's eastern quest, but made it clear that he must pursue that quest without creating ill will amongst his neighbors.

"You are a true and noble friend, Henry," the king said to him. "You have spent all of your years in battle, always for the betterment of the fatherland. I bid you good fortune in your venture east, to once more drive away the heathens, and as a sign of goodwill I am lending you the Holy Lance."

Henry accepted the spear, but although a Christian, he did not believe in its power, and he was not satisfied with the king's offer. "I see black for you," Henry snarled faintly, so that none could hear, as the king turned and walked away. He uttered not another word about his state of discontent, and over the coming months he allowed his anger to fester.

Forsaken by God

Rebellion again broke out in Italy, and once more Lombardy was the site of the trouble. Having been thoroughly dominated by the Germanic knights for the last two decades, the Lombards slowly but successfully built a formidable army.

As he had done four times before, Frederick yet again called upon his knights to join him on a crusade into Italy, to put down the Lombard revolt. However, he had lost so many of his best soldiers and generals in the plague that followed the last war, he had a hard time gathering a large enough force. When he arrived in Lombardy, he found himself greatly outnumbered. "What will you do?" his closest friend and advisor, Conrad of Feuchtwangen, asked him in private.

"I must in the face of a storm think, live, and die as a king," Frederick answered him.

Frederick did not sleep that night. When the sun arose the next morning, he sent Conrad on an urgent mission to find Henry the Lion and request his help in the battle against the Lombards. Always loyal, Conrad agreed, and took his fastest horse on a mission to Brunswick. When he arrived at the Lion's castle, he forwarded Frederick's sincere plea for help. Still seething, Henry refused, claiming that he was too old to go to war.

"Deceit sleeps with malice," Frederick said to himself when he heard the devastating news. "The Lord truly has forsaken me." Thus, Frederick was without his best knight and severely undermanned when he by chance, not by design, went to battle with the Lombards in the city of Legnano. He was also without the Holy Lance.

The Battle of Legnano commenced on May 29, 1176. The start of the fight was marked by another bad omen for the Teutons. Just after Frederick made his call for "Unity, Justice, and Freedom," an unusual occurrence took place.

Two white doves, signs of the Lord's blessings, flew in a circle just above the Carocium, the Lombards's cherished holy standard,[82] which they carried with them into battle on a wagon pulled by eight oxen.

One of the German noblemen pointed to them and yelled, "Frederick, look!" Seeing the doves circling above, the king said not a word, but his expression immediately turned from concerned to utterly grim.

Frederick and his knights were outnumbered more than four to one, but still it seemed in the beginning as if they had the upper hand, as they forcefully drove the Lombards backwards. Yet, it was an uphill battle. "For every ten we vanquished, twenty more took their place," one German knight later recounted the harrowing tale.

The Teutons may have yet carried the day had not two simultaneous devastating events occurred. The first was the loss of the German standard, the flag that symbolized the power and unity of the German knights. But the greater calamity was the fall of King Frederick in battle. A witness described the scene:

> When the Christian standard fell into the hands of the Lombards, King Frederick, clad in splendid armor, rushed against them at the head of a band of his chosen knights, But suddenly, he was seen to fall from his horse and vanish underneath the hot press of struggling warriors that surged back and forth around the standard. The dire event spread instant terror through the German ranks. They broke and fled, leaderless and in utter disorder.[83]

Battle of Legnano[84]

82 A standard is the flag or banner of an army or nation.
83 Adapted from Charles Morris' *Historical Tales: The Romance of Reality* (London: Gibbings & Co., 1894). http://fullreads.com/literature/frederick-barbarossa-and-milan/3/, retrieved 5-2-22.
84 https://commons.wikimedia.org/wiki/File:Battle_of_Legnano.png

Beatrice in Mourning

For three days Frederick was presumed dead, and his dutiful wife Beatrice wore the black robes of a widow in mourning. Deep despair overtook the German knights, who had retreated to Pavia. There were tears and sorrowful prayers, and the mood in the German camp could not have been more somber. For three days the sun did not shine. But on the fourth day, the king arrived unharmed and in good spirits. He had miraculously fought through the masses of Lombard warriors, and had found his way to safety.

The knights rejoiced when they saw their king alive and well, and Beatrice wept tears of joy. There were triumphant cries of "Long live the king!" heard all around. And the minstrels' remorseful songs quickly changed to songs of levity.

The Lombards, however, felt instant dread. They thought they had once and for all rid themselves of their noble foe, and were devastated to find out he lived. Their fear grew greater than it had ever been before, because they knew what type of man he was, and what he was capable of doing. They instantly began to negotiate a peace with the king, one very favorable to the German Empire. The king himself was greatly surprised by this. He found that he had gained as much through his skills as a politician and negotiator as he had hoped to gain in battle. "The Lord put me to the task, and by His grace I have endured," he proclaimed. "Thanks be to God!"

CHAPTER 15

Revenge Against Henry the Lion

Frederick had spent considerable time and energy in Italy, as he dreamed of becoming an all-powerful Holy Roman Emperor as the legendary King Otto the Great had been. However, he never before looked at what truly made Otto great. It wasn't his conquest of Rome, but rather his unification of the Germanic Empire, and the peace and prosperity that came with it, that made Otto a king of mythical proportion.

"Mine remains an empire divided," Frederick lamented. "I swear by my beard, I will make things right. Yesterday I was clever, so I wanted to change the world. Today I am wise, so I am changing myself."

From that moment on, Frederick dedicated his life to the betterment of his German homeland. First and foremost, there was the score to settle with Henry the Lion. The German Empire could never truly know peace, and truly prosper, as long as Henry defied the king and threatened his neighbors. Frederick issued a decree condemning his former comrade-in-arms of crimes against the Crown. In 1182, Henry the Lion was summoned to the Reichstag, a royal court, to answer the charges against him. His refusal brought from Frederick a declaration of the forfeiture of his estates.

Civil war broke out in the German Empire. As most of the German princes and dukes were chivalrous men of honor, they sided with their gallant king. Henry found that he had few friends and supporters, but he was brave, and was determined to put up a vigorous fight.

Although initially Henry found some success against his neighbors, in large part due to his military genius, he did not stand up well against the king and his royal knights. Frederick soon brought his army to the outskirts of Henry's well-fortified castle at Brunswick. Henry put on his best armor and grabbed his shield with the lion emblem. Although brave and not afraid to die, Henry did feel remorse that day. "Has ambition led me so far astray?" he murmured. "The king was always true. He has always treated me justly. Yet the die is cast. If the stars have so written, then I will die by his sword."

Standing in front of his army of knights on the grounds of Brunswick with stout posture and stern expression, Frederick called out more clearly and determinedly than he had ever done before, "Unity, Justice, and Freedom!"

A ferocious battle ensued on the grounds of Brunswick. In the end, Henry's forces were utterly crushed. Seeing all his ambitious hopes and dreams shattered, Henry recalled the ominous words of wisdom his father had imparted to him many years before—"Fear the reckoning of those you've wronged."

Exhausted and scarred, Henry dropped to his knees in front of Frederick. "Be merciful, my good king, and kill me quickly," he said with a heavy heart.

Frederick dismounted from his steed and drew his sword, advancing slowly towards Henry. The man known as the Lion expected to hear the king curse him. He expected expressions of rage. He expected the worst of all outcomes, but when he looked up he saw tears in Frederick's eyes. "I shall not kill you, brave knight . . . and friend," the king said to him. "It is not your destiny to die here. Yet, there must be justice."

There was justice. Henry's duchies of Saxony and Bavaria were divided into smaller fiefs, dependent on the king, and only two castles were left to him. As further punishment, Frederick banished him from the German Empire for the next three years. Henry went to live in his wife's kingdom in England, and every day missed his beloved homeland.

Having doled out the punishment, Frederick reclaimed the Holy Lance, and he never let it leave his side again. "I shall take it with me to the grave," Frederick said of the spear. "Heaven help us should it fall into the wrong hands."

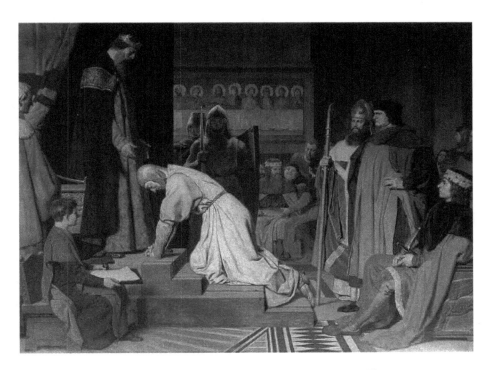

Henry the Lion bows before Frederick[85]

85 https://commons.wikimedia.org/wiki/File:FriedrichBarbarossa.jpg

CHAPTER 16

The Crusade Against the Slavs

Peace and prosperity returned to the confines of the German Empire, and it was a greater peace than it had ever known before or since. Frederick was beloved by all in his kingdom, and the bards sang his praises in every village and in the courtyards of every castle.

Having firmly secured peace at home, Frederick now looked to take the reins that had been held by Henry the Lion and venture even further to the east to help convert the pagan Slavs. There, in the lands across the Elbe, Frederick first met the remarkable seafaring Norsemen, of whom there was so much lore and legend that volumes could fill his castle library.

The Norseman

Having converted to Christianity, and given up their former ways of random pillage and plunder, the Norsemen took to new pursuits. There were many Scandinavian knights, the sons of converted Vikings, who joined in the crusade against the eastern Slavs. The bravest and boldest was a young knight named Vilhelm Johansson, Jarl of the Oaks, from Halland on the Sea of Kattegat. Vilhelm had served under the command of the famed Jarl Birgir Brosa, who kept peace in Sweden during the Scandinavian civil wars. There, Vilhelm learned to be a fine swordsman, and he never lost a duel.

Frederick met Vilhelm on an autumn day, after the Germanic knights had joined forces with the Norsemen to defeat the Slavic chieftain Slawomir. Frederick quickly befriended the young Hallander and was intrigued by his many Norse tales. The sagas of the Viking Ragnar Lothbrok were engrossing, but Frederick was most intrigued by the stories of a land far across the sea to the west.

"My great-great-grandfather served under a noble Jarl, named Leif," Vilhelm began. "Leif was the son of Erik the Red, a bold explorer with a mighty temper. Like his father, Leif was an adventurous sailor. One day Leif, with my forefather in his crew, set sail from Iceland to a port in Greenland, but a great storm blew them off course. Days later they spotted land, far to the west. It was inhabited by a tribe of dark-skinned warriors who they called Skraelings. The land itself they referred to as Vinland, for many grapes grew on the vines there. It was a beautiful land that stretched as far as the eye can see. I hope to venture there myself someday."

Leif Erikson in the New World[86]

"The greatest and noblest pleasure which we have in this world is to discover new truths. Someday, if the Good Lord agrees, I too would like to visit this Vinland," Frederick told him. "Yet I am getting long in the tooth, and I may not have many adventures left in my future."

Vilhelm and Frederick fought many battles against the Slavs together, and they were always victorious. Even on the darkest and coldest days of winter, they fearlessly fought. Vilhelm seemed immune to the cold. "There is no bad weather, only bad clothing," he would often proclaim. Frederick agreed, and he himself avidly adopted the saying.

In the spring of the following year, Frederick offered Vilhelm a position in his court at Hohenstaufen Castle once the wars in the east ended. Vilhelm accepted, for he admired the king's righteousness and chivalrous nature. Yet, it was not to be. One day Vilhelm received word from his elderly father. Their village in Halland had come under attack from a band of pagan Berserkers. "I must go and defend my homeland," he said.

"The wheel of fortune is forever in motion," the king replied. "Godspeed."

Before Vilhelm packed his belongings and left on his long journey, the king called all of his nobles to gather round, and knighted Vilhelm. "Will you, Vilhelm Johansson, take the oath of knighthood?" the king asked him as Vilhelm knelt before him.

"I will," he answered.

"Do you vow to always speak the truth?"

"I do."

---

86 https://commons.wikimedia.org/wiki/File:Leif_Erikson_Discovers_America_Hans_Dahl.jpg

"Do you vow to always defend the dignity of a lady?"

"I do."

"Do you vow to be loyal to the Church, and always devoted to God?"

"I do."

"Do you vow to be charitable?"

"I do."

"Do you vow to always be brave?"

"I do."

"Do you vow to defend the poor and the helpless?"

"I do."

The king then dubbed him, announcing to all, "I knight thee, Herr Vilhelm. Now go and do God's will in my name." Frederick gave Vilhelm his silver sword, the one he had used to slay the great wolf. "Save your people from the pagans," the king said to him.

"Thank you, your majesty," he replied. "It has been a true honor to serve with you. You have been a mentor and an inspiration. When I return to Halland, I will tell my people the tales of your adventures, and of your goodwill and kingly righteousness." Vilhelm then mounted his horse and rode furiously to the north.

Ivan the Giant

Frederick continued the crusade to the east of the Elbe without his Norseman comrades. Soon he was to face one of his most noteworthy opponents. There was a giant among the Slavs named Ivan. His forefather was the famed warrior Vlad, who had met his fate in a duel with the legendary Gero at the Raxa in the year 955. Ivan was over seven feet tall, and would have been even taller had he not had a hunchback. He had a thick build and was as strong as an ox, but he lacked the natural aggression and battlefield acumen of his famous forefather. He was slow-witted and slow afoot, and he had a lazy eye that compromised his vision. Still, he wished to win the favor of his countrymen, and when he came of age at the time of Frederick's invasion into the eastern lands, he challenged the great king to a battle to the death. The courageous king was getting old, but he still was a magnificent warrior, and he feared no one, not even a hulking giant.

"We can fight with the weapon of your choosing," the king said to Ivan.

"With spears," the giant grunted.

"So be it," the king agreed, and he walked back to his horse and grabbed the Holy Lance.

Although weak-minded, the giant believed he had the upper hand, because the pagan high priest from his village had given him the Spear of Perun, a weapon said to have been forged with celestial fire by the Slavic God of War. "He who carries it shall smite his enemy," the high priest had told him. Knights and barbarians together gathered round to witness the great battle that was about to unfold.

Although lacking quickness and agility, the giant had a much further reach. Still, the king had far greater experience in battle, and he had no doubt that he would succeed. After an initial period of sizing each other up, the king lashed out first and struck the shaft of the giant's spear with the blade of the Holy Lance. The battle was over before it began, because the giant's weapon shattered into seven pieces, and Ivan was left defenseless.

The king could see the fear overtake the young Slav. "You should listen when an old dog barks," Frederick said to him. "You are not a fighter. You, I can see, are a man of peace. My God is the king of peace. Join me and give yourself to Christ, and I promise you will never need fight again. You will never see blood spilled. You will rejoice with every sunrise, and find tranquility with every sunset."

The giant converted that day, and was warmly embraced by the German knights. True to his word, the king granted the giant a home to live in and land to farm, and never once called on him to bear arms.

CHAPTER 17

Hiedler and the Jews

At the time of the First Crusade in the late eleventh and early twelfth centuries, the fervor in Europe had led to an uprising against the Jews. Many Jews had their homes and property destroyed, and many were brutally murdered. Not wanting a repeat of the treachery in his kingdom, Frederick decreed that no unjust harm should be done to the Jews, under the penalty of death. Most followed the king's order, but there were areas within the empire that were so filled with hatred that the people there ignored the royal decree.

The most notorious of the villains was a duke named Heinrich Hiedler from Prounaw, on the lower river Inn, east of Munich and north of Salzburg. He was a verbose man with uncontrollable emotions and a crazed look about him. He had delusions of grandeur, and dressed in shining armor when he ventured out of his castle, even though Prounaw was not at war. Filled with hatred, he rounded up all the Jews in his dukedom, and also kidnapped them from the surrounding cities and villages. He made the Jews into slaves, even the children, and ordered that they only be given enough daily rations to keep from starving to death, although many did starve. Many more died from disease as they were housed in horrid, filthy conditions.

Heinrich Hiedler[87]

---

87 https://commons.wikimedia.org/wiki/File:Hubert_Lanzinger_Der_Bannertr%C3%A4ger_(The_Standard_bearer)_1934-36_Adolf_Hitler_Postkarte_Ansichtskarte_Photo-Hoffmann_M%C3%BCnchen_Card_no._428_NSDAP_Propaganda_Knight_in_armour_Nazi_postcard_Swastika_flag_No_known_copyright_restrictions.jpg

Oskar Moltke, a pious Christian man from Prounaw, one of the few who had not left after Hiedler took control, traveled a great way to inform the king of the abominable sins being committed in his village.

Intolerant of injustice, Frederick and twelve of his bravest knights set out at once for Prounaw. It was typically a three-day journey by horseback, but they made it in two. When they arrived in the village, they came upon the labor camp where Hiedler had imprisoned the Jews. Frederick immediately became enraged, as there was a carved sign there, arched over the gait at the camp entrance, which appallingly read "LABOR FOR BARBAROSSA."

"How dare he use my name!" the king roared. He dismounted his steed, picked up a rock, and hurled it with fury at the sign. He then picked up another and did the same. He looked for a third but could find none. "How dare he use my name!" he roared again. The king then grabbed a battle axe from a brave knight named Dietrich, and rushed with it towards the gate. His loyal knights had never before seen him so impassioned.

"Woe to this villain once the king apprehends him," one knight said. "He will wish he had never been born."

"God may have mercy," said another, "but the king will not."

"Let there be justice for the wicked," said a third.

All twelve stood in awe of their righteous leader.

"How dare he use my name!" Barbarossa roared for a third time, even louder than before. His thunderous voice could be heard echoing off the nearby highlands. Frederick, with all his might, took the axe and ardently destroyed the unholy gate and the irreverent wooden sign that stood over it.

Having razed the entrance to the camp, Frederick and his knights immediately freed the Jews, many of whom were no more than skin and bone, all of whom were forlorn and hopeless. "Has there ever before been so much evil in the soul of one man?" Frederick questioned as he saw with his own eyes the horrid conditions in the camp.

Moltke led Frederick and the knights to Hiedler's castle. Unlike the rest of his dukedom, which was dreary and dilapidated, his castle and its grounds were immaculate. The beauty there rivaled that of the Hohenstaufen estate. "Bring the monster to me!" Frederick charged. He was so angry that his face was nearly as red as his beard. "Death to the wolf will be life to the lambs!"

The knights stormed the castle, bound the villain, and dragged him kicking and screaming like a lunatic in front of the king. When Hiedler saw that he was in the presence of Frederick, he initially became silent.

"Hiedler," the king said to the anti-Semite, "look upon the beautifully lit sky, with the sun in all its glory. For after today you will never see it again.

"And look upon the glorious fields of the Lord, the magnificent mountains and valleys, and take in the wonder, for after the sun sets tonight, they will be forever gone to you.

"And hear the lovely songs of the birds, singing the praises of God, for it is the last day you'll ever hear such sweet sound.

"And smell the fresh fragrance of the flowers, for after today you'll smell nothing but death forevermore.

"Hiedler, you are a demon, and on this day I banish you to the eternal fires of Hell."

Hiedler clenched his teeth in rage, his maddened eyes widened, and he broke his silence. "You may kill me, but my blood lives on, and I will have my day against the Jews. I swear an oath this shall come to pass, and the Kingdom of Germany will suffer like never before because of your foolishness." They were the last words he ever spoke.

Hiedler was unmercifully beaten and executed by hanging on the thirteenth day of the month. The sun was a quarter of the way above the western horizon when the noose was placed around his neck. The weather could not have been more perfect. But at the moment he took his last gasp, the sky suddenly turned as dark as night, and only a faint halo of light could be seen around the blackened orb in the late afternoon sky.

"It is an omen," the peasants cried, and they ran to their homes in terror. The Jews who had just been freed huddled on the ground, covered their faces, and shook with fear. Even the knights, as brave as they were, trembled.

"Lord have mercy on our people," King Frederick called out in the darkness. He then dropped to his knees in prayer and looked upwards toward Heaven. He prayed fervently and within minutes the light was restored, but all remained shaken from the events of the day. Some remained shaken for weeks, some for months, and some for many years.

The forlorn Jews of the region, the ones who were strong enough to travel, eventually migrated to the north and east, hoping to find greater peace in the land of the Slavs.

CHAPTER 18
The Battle of Iconium

Late in the twelfth century, there were two great and powerful Muslim states, the Sultanate of Rum[88] and the Ayyubid Sultanate.[89] They lived at peace with the Christian Kingdom of Jerusalem, allowing Christian pilgrims safe passage to and from the Holy Lands; and in return, the Christians allowed safe passage for the Muslim travelers in their lands. The Sultan of Ayyubid was named Saladin. He was a noble man and a brilliant leader, who was in many ways as chivalrous as the Christian kings of the era. He at times corresponded with King Frederick, and they had great respect for one another.

The peace between Christians and Muslims was shattered, however, in the year 1187. Raynald of Chatillon, a rogue French knight, committed an audaciously violent act by robbing Saladin's mother of her treasures while she was passing through Jerusalem, and killing her attendants.[90] Saladin retaliated by invading Jerusalem. He routed the Christian army in the Battle of Hattin and had Raynald of Chatillon beheaded. The victorious Saracens tore down the crosses from Christian churches, and assembled for prayer in the Temple of Solomon.

Saladin[91]

---

88 Present-day Turkey.
89 Present-day Egypt.
90 Kuhn, *Barbarossa*.
91 https://commons.wikimedia.org/wiki/File:Saladin_enters_Jerusalem.jpg

Upon hearing the news of the fall of Jerusalem to the Saracens, Pope Gregory VIII, in the bull[92] *Audita tremendi*, called for a new crusade. King Henry II of England[93] and King Phillip II of France heeded the call. Being the elder Christian statesman of Europe, and the one with the most military experience, Frederick felt it was his duty to also join the crusade, but he did so with some reluctance, given his cordial relationship with Saladin. In an act of goodwill, he wrote a lengthy letter to the sultan, explaining his decision to go to war against him, and paradoxically wishing him well.

Frederick gathered together a large army of Teutonic knights, far larger than that of the French or English. He was also far more organized than his co-crusaders. In 1189, Frederick and his men set out to the Holy Land. He chose the longer land route to get there, rather than travel by ship, for he never forgot the siren's prophecy of his death in a watery grave.

Sir Robert of Loxley

When Frederick and his army were a two-day journey outside of Constantinople, they encountered a small group of knights who appeared Northern European rather than Byzantine. This puzzled the Germans, as although both France and England had joined the crusade against Saladin, neither the king of France nor of England had set out for Jerusalem yet. The leader of the group was clad in green, and appeared to be an archer. He addressed the king in a Saxon dialect that Frederick had only heard spoken a few times before, but the king was still able to understand,

"I am Sir Robert Hode, of the province of Loxley in England. My men and I are loyal subjects of King Richard the Lionheart," the green-clad knight proclaimed. "King Richard sent us here to scout the Saracen forces, so that we may report back to him as soon as he arrives."

"You are welcome to join us," Frederick offered.

"We would be honored to do so," Sir Robert replied.

Camping together, the English and German knights exchanged tales, and Frederick soon learned that Sir Robert was the greatest archer in all of England. Being a gifted archer himself, the king challenged him to a friendly contest. "Let us stand thirty yards from a target, and see which of us comes closest to the bullseye," the king suggested.

"I would be delighted to partake," Sir Robert said.

Many knights quickly gathered to see the two duel. After each took several practice shots, the king was first to the challenge. Standing exactly thirty yards from a circular wooden shield hung on a tree, he pulled back the bowstring and let loose. His shot was perfect—right in the middle of the target, not even a half an inch off. The German knights wildly cheered their king.

---

92 A bull is an official edict from the pope.
93 King Henry died before the actual crusade began, and was replaced by King Richard the Lionheart.

Sir Robert Hode[94]

"I think I was a little lucky," the king graciously said to Sir Robert.

"It was a magnificent shot, Your Majesty," Sir Robert replied. "The finest I've ever seen in all my days. There is no way to top that."

Nevertheless, Sir Robert took his turn. He studied the target, pulled back the bowstring and unleashed the arrow with great speed. Sir Robert's arrow struck the back end of Frederick's and ricocheted away, missing the target completely.

94 https://commons.wikimedia.org/wiki/File:Louis_Rhead_Robin_Hood.jpg

Again the German knights cheered as the king had won. Frederick, however, being a masterful archer, fully appreciated the incredible skill exhibited by Sir Robert. To be able to hit the back end of his arrow was the work of a genius. "I'm afraid your luck was as bad as mine was good," the king said to Sir Robert. "Let us have one more go at it."

This time the Englishman went first. He was a chivalrous man and did not want to spoil the king's fair-natured proposal to partake in another round. So, he missed the center of the target on purpose by a mere two inches. *It is enough to allow the king to win, but not far enough off that the king should suspect anything,* Sir Robert surmised.

The latter part of Sir Robert's assumption was incorrect. King Frederick immediately suspected that he had missed on purpose, and being a chivalrous man himself, he purposefully missed just two inches to the side of Sir Robert's shot, making Sir Robert the victor.

The competition was all in good fun, and the men celebrated that night before continuing on with their crusade the next morning. The King placed Sir Robert and his men under the command of his eldest son, Frederick IV, together with a group of knights led by a young duke named Albrecht of Hohenzollern. Albrecht was the best of the German archers, and had much in common with Sir Robert, not only in terms of battle skills but in wisdom and righteousness. They would prove to be great allies in the upcoming hostilities against the Saracens.

Before venturing onward, the king gave some words of advice to Sir Robert, who was many years his younger. "The greatest danger for most of us is not that our aim is too high and we miss it, but that it is too low and we reach it. Be bold, dear Robert. Live fully. You have great talents. Put them to use so that long after you are gone from this earth, men will remember your name."

The Silver Ransom

Travelling through Byzantium, just as in the Second Crusade, the German knights were met with hostility from their fellow Christians, but they eventually made it to the Saltanate of Rum, through which they had to pass to reach the Kingdom of Jerusalem. The Saracens raided the Crusaders as they marched along. The hit-and-run raids were most often nothing more than a nuisance, but there were two occasions where they proved especially difficult. The first was when the brave German knights marched through a valley and soon found themselves surrounded by their enemy on the hills above. The high ground gave the Saracens a great advantage.

"We must turn away and find a safer passage," a Christian nobleman said to Frederick. "It may delay us, but it will save many lives."

"What he says is true," another nobleman, riding a stately white horse, agreed. "It is the prudent thing to do."

"Only dead fish follow the stream," Frederick answered them, indicating his determination to stay on course no matter how difficult.

The Saracen warriors, although angered by the foreigners in their homeland, were far more interested in gold and silver than they were military victories, and offered to let the Crusaders pass unharmed for a hefty fee. They sent a ransom note by messenger to King Frederick. Reading the note, the noble king laughed. He placed a single small silver coin in a cloth sack and gave it to the Saracen messenger. "Here is your ransom," the king wrote back to them. "Split it amongst yourselves." The German knights then went on to vanquish their foes in battle, despite their enemy having the higher ground.

The second occasion was when the Teutons came to a narrow bridge, heavily defended by fierce Arabian knights. Again, rather than fight, the Saracens looked to make a profit, and offered safe passage for the Christians for the proper fee. They demanded 300 pounds of gold, and the lands of the Armenians.

Barbarossa refused, proclaiming, "Rather than making a royal highway with gold and silver, with the help of our Lord Jesus Christ, whose knights we are, the road will have to be opened with iron."[95]

Again, the Christians routed their enemy and passed the bridge. Yet despite the heroic triumph, there was no joy that day for the king, for his loyal friend Conrad of Feuchtwangen fell in battle, wounded in the neck by a Turk's sword. A fellow knight recorded the sadness of the day:

> They had laid their dear one under a great oak tree, which extended its branches over him like protecting arms, and sought to stanch his wound. The sight bitterly grieved the King as he approached. He had found the steed and shield of his old comrade-in-arms, and well knew what he had lost; but the spot showed clearly what his life had cost the enemy, for the shield was covered with blood and a wall of slain lay beside it. He at once ordered that his brave friend should be taken to his own tent and cared for as such a friend deserved. "Were it possible to purchase thy life, thou faithful one, I would give this day's honor," said the King, with great emotion.[96]

Conrad did not survive his wound. His pulse grew faint and his breathing shallow. His vision dimmed. His last words were these: "I die willingly, for my King and my God."

Frederick knelt by his friend's side and placed his hand on his shoulder. With tear-filled eyes he said, "Ashes to ashes, and dust to dust. Go forth in peace, for you have followed the good road. Go forth without fear, for He that created you loves you." Then they buried him with much sorrow.

95 Wikipedia, "Battle of Iconium." https://en.wikipedia.org/wiki/Battle_of_Iconium_(1190), retrieved 4-12-22.
96 Kuhn, *Barbarossa.*

Conrad's Sons

Not long thereafter, when the Crusaders were just a three-day journey from the great Saracen city of Iconium, the noble sons of Conrad of Feuchtwangen, still grieving over the death of their father, were ambushed and kidnapped by the enemy. The sons were named Raymond and Conrad II. They were chivalrous knights with brave hearts, but they were outnumbered by far too many Turks to battle their way to safety.

Noting that the two knights were the sons of a high ranking noble and friend of the king, the Saracens did not kill them but rather imprisoned them in an impenetrable fortress. The fortress was on a large estate surrounded by high walls. Inside the walls, the sultan had collected the most dangerous beasts from the African continent, and dispersed them throughout so no man or army could pass unharmed. The Saracens had a mile-long tunnel underneath the grounds of the fortress, which allowed them to traverse the dangerous area; but the tunnel was well-hidden, and the Crusaders knew not of its existence.

The king was occupied planning the momentous upcoming battle, but, loving Conrad's sons as his own, he sent a group of ten of his bravest knights to rescue the captured brothers. To his chagrin, the ten came back with wounds and fear in their hearts, for the beasts were so ferocious that they did not even make it thirty yards after scaling the wall.

"I have faced greater beasts than these," the king said. "I will go alone and free the boys." The king then looked towards the heavens and addressed his old friend. "Conrad, I swear by my beard, I shall not fail."

Frederick grabbed the Holy Lance as his only weapon and rode on his trusty horse to the outskirts of the fortress. He climbed the wall and soon encountered a giant tiger. The tiger roared at him, but Frederick raised the Holy Lance, and the beast became subdued and laid gently on the ground in front of him. So it was for all the fearsome beasts that the king encountered on his way to the fortress.

Frederick then went up to the fortress gate, shattered the lock with his spear, and called out to the young knights. When they ran to the entryway, they were shocked to see that it was their king, standing alone, who had come to save them.

The Charge of the White Knights

On May 18, 1190, the great Battle of Iconium commenced. Frederick split his army of knights in two. His son Frederick IV, Duke of Swabia, led one half, and the king himself led the other. They engaged a force of battle-hardened Saracens far larger than their own. Much was at stake, for the victor would control the entire Sultanate of Rum. The Saracens were led by the bloodthirsty Qutb al-Din, the son of the Sultan of Rum.

"We shall wipe the Christian menace from the face of the earth," Qutb al-Din proclaimed to his army. "Not one shall escape our wrath! Behead them all! Behead their soldiers, behead their priests, and behead the maids and squires that accompany and serve them." Qutb al-Din then turned to his chancellor and added, "I myself shall behead their king. A head stuck on a pike no longer conspires."

The day before the great battle, Frederick had his knights encamp in the expansive Garden of the Sultan, just outside the city limits, where the water was plentiful. Early on the morning of the eighteenth, Qutb al-Din, clad all in black, led a vicious attack against the Christians. The Muslims shouted "Allah" as they charged with swiftness and ferocity. While Qutb al-Din battled the king's forces in the field, the king's son, accompanied by Sir Robert and Albrecht, captured the city with relative ease, and raised the banner of the Holy Roman Empire. Despite the raising of the noble double-headed eagle flag, the battle was far from over. The Christians in the field, facing Qutb al-Din and his main forces, were having a hard time of it. There were three Saracens for every German knight, and initially it appeared that the Muslims would be victorious; but then Frederick raised the Holy Lance high above his head and cried out, "Christ reigns! Christ conquers! Christ commands!"

With that call, the king sent forth into battle his most elite warriors, who he had previously held in reserve. At once, thousands of heavily armored Teutonic knights, cloaked in pure white tunics, save the black crosses on their chests, rode snow-white clad horses into battle against the beastlike army of Qutb al-Din. These were stout-hearted, God-fearing men, loyal to the death, and personally chosen and trained by the king himself. They were the most honorable and chivalrous in all the land. They stormed in like a shimmering army of God, with the Middle Eastern sun's rays illuminating them in all their glory. With their silver swords and iron spears, they utterly routed the Saracens, who either fell woefully in the field or retreated in abject fear.

Qutb al-Din's advisors, shamed by the humiliating defeat, mutinied and executed their leader. They placed his head on a pike among the thousands of dead. They then took their own lives by the sword, crying out "Allah forgive us" in their final moments.

For all his many accomplishments, and for all the battles he had fought, the king was never as proud as he was that day. He had never before witnessed an army fight with the brilliance displayed by the white knights at Iconium. None ever had. His feelings stood in stark contrast to those of his noble foe. In his far-away castle, Saladin was stricken with fear when he heard of the plight of Qutb al-Din and his Saracen warriors. "What have I wrought upon my people?" the Sultan cried. His hands trembled and he gnashed his teeth.

Painting of the Battle of Iconium[97]

---

97 https://commons.wikimedia.org/wiki/File:Barbarossas_Sieg_bei_Ikonium.jpg

CHAPTER 19

Death in the River

Death smiles at us all. All a man can do is smile back.
—Marcus Aurelius

After their great victory at Iconium, Frederick and his army ventured onward toward Jerusalem. He wanted to avoid a long march in the dreadful heat and also wished to avoid the mountain peaks, so he took the advice of the Armenians and chose a shortcut along the River Saleph in Asia Minor. It was along this route that death smiled upon him. The fateful moment arrived without the glory that warriors seek in battle. It arrived clandestinely, without a chance for farewells.

It was a gray, humid day, with a subtle fog. There was a single bridge over the Saleph, and the road leading up to it was encumbered with cattle. The king was impatient in the brutal midday heat and, against the advice of his supporters, he drove his steed across the rapids. Just before he did, he noticed two jet-black ravens circling overhead. The dour birds distracted him, and when his horse slipped on a wet stone, he dropped the Holy Lance into the rushing water. A moment later, the king himself was dragged under the torrential stream. He struggled at first, but his struggle was brief, and as Lorelei had prophesized years before, he met his death in a watery grave. Many of his accompanying knights tried to rush in to save him, but their efforts were all in vain. The king was sixty-seven years old. The date was June 10th, 1190.

Raymond, Conrad's noble son who was traveling with Frederick, later recorded the event:

Frederick's son led the first group of knights across the narrow bridge. There was a mass of men waiting to cross. Becoming impatient, the King now prepared to follow. Without heeding the advice of his attendants, the aged hero, who had never known what fear meant, put spurs to his steed, and plunged with him into the waters of the Saleph. For a few seconds the golden armor gleamed amid the waves, once or twice the reverend, hoary head rose above the stream, then the deadly waters carried horse and rider into their raging depths, and the beloved hero vanished from the eyes of his sorrowing army. His most valiant knights indeed and chosen friends plunged after him into the flood to save their honored prince or die with him, but the wild mountain torrent bore them all to death. With bitter lamentations the army wandered up and down the stream, if perchance they might at least win the precious corpse from the waters. But night came and threw its dark veil over the sorrow and mourning of the day.[98]

---

98 Kuhn, *Barbarossa.*

CHAPTER 20

The Kyffhäuser Mountains

The ancient Barbarossa,
Frederick, the Kaiser great,
Within the castle-cavern
Sits in enchanted state.

He did not die; but ever
Waits in the chamber deep,
Where hidden under the castle
He sat himself to sleep.

The splendor of the Empire
He took with him away,
And back to earth will bring it
When dawns the promised day.

The chair is ivory purest
Whereof he makes his bed;
The table is of marble
Whereon he props his head.

His beard, not flax, but burning
With fierce and fiery glow,
Right through the marble table
Beneath his chair does grow.

He nods in dreams and winketh
With dull, half-open eyes,
And once a page he beckons--
A page that standeth by.

He bids the boy in slumber
"O dwarf, go up this hour,
And see if still the ravens
Are flying round the tower;

And if the ancient ravens
Still wheel above us here,
Then must I sleep enchanted
For many a hundred year."[99]

—Friedrich Ruckert (1788-1866)

99 https://allpoetry.com/Barbarossa, retrieved 5-19-2022

Frederick Barbarossa in the Kyffhäuser Mountains[100]

---

100 https://commons.wikimedia.org/wiki/File:KaempfferRotbart.jpg

Back in the German Empire, many refused to believe that the king was dead. He was so beloved, and he seemed so strong, full of life, and graced by God, that many rejected the claim. "They said he was dead before, at Legnano, and yet he lived," many pointed out. "He surely lives on still."

One of the greatest doubters was the king's bard and poet in Swabia, a man named Anselm. Having heard the king's tale of his meeting with the siren Lorelei, and having retold it himself on many occasions, Anselm set out to the Rhine to find the mysterious woman. "Surely she will know the truth," he said.

Anselm was not certain if Lorelei still lived, and he expected to find an elderly woman if he found her at all. But when he reached the banks of the Rhine, near the large bluff in the area called the Rhine Gorge, he met a beautiful woman with golden hair. She was neither young nor old. She sat on the rock in the river, just several feet from the bank. "Are you the maiden Lorelei?" Anselm called out to her.

"I am," she answered.

"I am Anselm from Swabia, a humble servant of our good King Frederick. I beseech thee to help me."

"I will help you if I can."

"Is what they say true?" Anselm asked. "Is our noble king today with Christ in heaven? Forever gone from this realm?

"The king has fulfilled his destiny. He is not in Heaven, but he has gone from this realm," Lorelei answered him.

The poet was confused. "Where is he, then?"

"The king and his bravest soldiers were led far away, past the Gold Meadows to the Kyff-häuser Mountains, and there in a deep cave, hidden far from sight, they will remain until the ravens cease to fly."

"Is he imprisoned?"

"No, far from it," she said. "He is filled with bliss, for upon entering the cave he found his beloved Gela waiting for him. And together they rest and keep watch."

"Until the ravens cease to fly? What does that mean?" the poet questioned.

"I have no more to say," Lorelei said. She then dove from the rock into the waters of the Rhine, and disappeared into the mist.

"Lorelei, come back!" the poet shouted out. "Please, Lorelei! There is so much more I need to know."

The maiden never did return. She was never seen again.

Anselm stared out at the Rhine for a moment, hypnotized by its beauty in the mist. He then turned away, mounted his steed and returned to his humble home in Swabia. After a few days passed, while sitting quietly alone by a gentle fire, he recorded the final account of the Red-Bearded King.

Barbarossa's youthful dream was fulfilled. Gela, his first love, was now at his side to tend him and bless him forever as she could never have done on earth. It was she, the faithful one, who ruled henceforth in the magic kingdom of the Kyffhäuser, and cared for the beloved hero and his trusty band. It was she who knew when Barbarossa's heart yearned over the memories of his glorious past. Then she would lead the knights—his faithful comrades in the Holy War—into his room. They would range themselves round the marble table at which Barbarossa sat, with his long red beard flowing round him like imperial ermine, and over the golden goblets, filled from the exhaustless stores of the mountain cellars, they talked with the hero about the glorious days that they had spent together, about "the golden age" of the Holy German Empire. And the minstrels, who had been wont to go with him to the Holy Land, and had entered with him the enchanted mountain of the "Golden Meadow," would strike their harps, and the song of the future, which still slumbered in their souls, rose to their lips and echoed loudly through the enchanted arches of the Kyffhäuser Mountain.[101]

This was their song:

"Never let it be forgot, no matter how many years may pass, that for one brief shining moment, here on this blessed patch of earth, there was justice and goodness for all, by the virtue of a king, a noble king, called Barbarossa."

---

101 https://www.gutenberg.org/files/39560/39560-h/39560-h.htm, downloaded 3-28-22

Monument to Frederick Barbarossa in the Kyffhäuser Mountains[102]

102 https://commons.wikimedia.org/wiki/File:Monument_barbarossa.jpg

Author's Notes

Although this book is a work of fiction, many of the characters and events are historical. Frederick Barbarossa really was a German king in the twelfth century. He was considered chivalrous in his time. He did indeed rid his land of many unscrupulous robber barons. He forbade persecution of the Jews prior to the Third Crusade. He enacted the Peace of the Land, creating a just system of governance, and he was generally loved by his people. Not only that, but Frederick actually possessed a spear that he believed was the Holy Lance (the spear used by Longinus to pierce the side of Christ). Today that spear resides on display in the Imperial Treasury at the Hofburg Palace in Vienna, Austria. Of note is that in the nineteenth century, Napoleon Bonaparte gained possession of the spear, as did Adolf Hitler in the twentieth century.

Unlike the case with the legendary Arthur, we know exactly where the German "Camelot" once stood. Frederick's castle (the Hohenstaufen Castle) was destroyed in the German Peasants War in the year 1525, but its ruins remain on a high hill overlooking the surrounding country-side. It can be visited in Goppingen, in Baden-Wurttemberg, Germany. I have not yet been, but it is high on my bucket list.

As written in this book, Frederick did lead a large army of German knights on the Third Crusade against Saladin, and he did die in the Saleph River (currently called the Goksu River). After his death, many of the German knights turned back and headed home. Richard the Lionheart of England and his former foe, the French king Philip II, took over command of the Christian forces, and although they met some success, they ultimately failed in their quest to regain Jerusalem. Thus, the battle-tested German king's untimely death on that fateful day in June likely changed the course of history for centuries to come.

There is a memorial to Frederick Barbarossa that can be visited in the Kyffhäuser Mountains in Thuringia, Germany, near Bad Frankenhausen. It was erected in the late nineteenth century. Around that same time, a deep cave was discovered in the mountains, which added to the romantic folklore.

Finally, I'd like to note that the chapter entitled "Hiedler and the Jews" is purely fictional. Although Barbarossa did, by royal decree, protect the Jews in Germany at the onset of the Third Crusade, there was no such man named Heinrich Hiedler.[103] However, in the year 1941, Adolf Hitler, a notoriously evil man, did use the name "Barbarossa" when he code-named the Nazi invasion of the Soviet Union "Operation Barbarossa." Because of this, the chivalrous medieval king, by no fault of his own, has unfortunately been associated with Hitler. Knowing that he was a man of deep faith, and one who did not tolerate injustice in his kingdom, it is likely that Frederick Barbarossa would have been enraged had he known of the evil twentieth-century dictator. I tried to reflect this in the Hiedler chapter.

---

103   Some historians believe that the surname Hitler evolved from Hiedler.

Portrait of Frederick Barbarossa asleep in the Kyffhäuser Mountains[104]

104 https://commons.wikimedia.org/wiki/File:The_Sleep_of_Emperor_Frederick_Barbarossa_by_Carolsfeld.jpg

Insofar as our nation recalls its medieval history, the figure of Frederick Barbarossa stands in the foreground of its memory. Frederick's perfect frame contained an equally sublime soul. His knightly valor adorned his majesty not less than this valor ennobled him. He was a man of rare spiritual sensitivity, worthy in every way of his position. An understanding of power, something necessary to every ruler, was possessed by him to the highest degree. When all is said and done, Frederick, along with Otto the Great, was the greatest ruler our nation had in the Middle Ages.[105]

—Dietrich Schafer (German Historian) 1923

Statue of Kaiser Rotbart[106]

---

105 Adapted from John B. Freed, *Frederick Barbarossa, the Prince and Myth* (Yale University Press, 2016), introduction.
106 Photo by Peter Wittgens, https://commons.wikimedia.org/wiki/File:Barbarossa-vom-Wilkinus.JPG

Timeline

876	Henry the Fowler is born
912	Otto I (the Great) is born
919	Henry is crowned King of Germany
933	Battle of Riade; the Germanic knights defeat the Magyars
936	Henry dies and Otto I becomes king
955	Battle of Lechfeld; Otto I saves Christendom from the pagan Magyars
955	Battle on the Raxa; Otto I defeats the pagan Slavs
962	Otto I becomes Holy Roman Emperor
963	Otto I conquers Rome
973	Otto I dies
1122	Frederick Barbarossa is born
1147	The start of the Second Crusade in the Holy Land
1152	Frederick is crowned King of Germany
1155	Frederick razes Tortona
1155	Frederick is crowned Holy Roman Emperor
1155	Frederick puts down the Roman revolt on the day of his coronation
1156	Frederick returns to Germany and enacts the Peace of the Land
1156	Frederick marries Beatrice of Burgundy
1158	Frederick together with Henry the Lion return to Italy and capture Milan
1158	Humiliation of Beatrice in Milan
1159	Frederick sacks Crema
1162	Rebellion in Milan
1162	Frederick razes Milan
1164-66	Frederick works for reforms in Germany
1166	Frederick returns to Italy to put down an uprising
1167	The great Germanic victory at Monte Porzio
1167	The plague (malaria) strikes the German knights and Frederick has to flee back to Germany
1176	The Battle of Legnano
1180	Frederick invades Saxony
1181	Henry the Lion is exiled from Germany for three years
1189	The start of the third Crusade
1190	Battle of Iconium on May 18
1190	Frederick drowns in the Saleph on June 10

Glossary

Adelaide: Otto the Great's beautiful and good-natured wife. She was later canonized by Pope Urban II in 1097.

Battle of Iconium: a battle in the Third Crusade in the year 1190. It was a heroic victory for the crusaders over the Turks.

Battle of Lechfeld: the epic battle in the year 955 that forever stalled the Magyar invasion into central Europe, thus saving Christendom.

Beatrice of Burgundy: Frederick Barbarossa's wife. She was beautiful, wise, and wealthy.

Conrad of Feuchtwangen: a legendary Teutonic knight and friend of Frederick Barbarossa.

Conrad the Red: a brave knight from Lorraine who fought alongside Otto I at Lechfeld.

Frederick I Barbarossa: a red-bearded, chivalrous twelfth century German king and Holy Roman Emperor.

Gela: the mythical love interest of the young Frederick Barbarossa.

Gero the Great: a heroic German knight in the tenth century.

Hartmann von Siebenneichen: Frederick Barbarossa's doppelganger.

Henry I (the Fowler): the first true king of the German Empire.

Henry the Lion: Duke of Saxony and Bavaria in the twelfth century. He was a great warrior.

Saint Hildegard of Bingen: a Benedictine abbess who was a writer, composer, philosopher, and mystic.

Hohenstaufen: a powerful royal family in medieval Germany.

Konrad III: the king of Germany who preceded Frederick Barbarossa.

Krampus: a mythical evil Christmas spirit in German folklore.

Kyffhäuser Mountains: a mountain range in central Germany. According to legend, Frederick Barbarossa sleeps in a deep cave here, and will reemerge one day when the ravens cease to fly.

Lorelei: a mythical siren on the Rhine River.

Otto I (the Great): a tenth century German king and Holy Roman Emperor. He was a highly successful military commander.

Rainald of Dassel: a brave German knight and Frederick Barbarossa's wise chancellor.

Raymond: a mythical Germanic knight, son of Conrad of Feuchtwangen, who went on crusade with Frederick Barbarossa.

References

Bob Stewart, *Barbarossa: Scourge of Europe*, Firebird Books, 1988.

David A. Warner, *Ottonian Germany: The Chronicon of Thietmar of Merseburg*, Manchester University Press, 2001.

Ernest F. Henderson, *A History of Germany in the Middle Ages*, George Bell and Sons, 1894.

Franz Kuhn, *Barbarossa*, George Putnam, 1906.

John B. Freed, *Frederick Barbarossa, the Prince and Myth*, Yale University Press, 2016.

Villamaria, *Fairy Circles: Tales and Legends*, Marcus Ward & Co., 1877.

Wikipedia, entries on "Frederick I, Holy Roman Emperor" and "Otto the Great."